P9-DFZ-148

"I can feel you tremble, Gemma."

Shade watched her closely as he spoke, and a leaping flame lit his eyes.

"How arrogant you are!" Gemma snapped. "If I tremble it's because I'm annoyed with you, not because I've fallen under your spell."

He lifted one dark eyebrow. "Annoyed with me? But why?"

"Because you won't take me seriously when I tell you I've no intention of getting involved...."

"Suppose I kiss all this nonsense away?" he said suddenly, his voice deep and vibrant.

For long moments she thought she hadn't heard him properly. There was an extended silence during which she felt his grip tighten on her shoulders. Then hysteria and some other emotion rose within her and she laughed nervously. "You wouldn't dare!"

"No?" he murmured, challengingly.

WELCOME
TO THE WONDERFUL WORLD
OF *Harlequin Romances*

Interesting, informative and entertaining,
each Harlequin Romance portrays an appealing
and original love story. With a varied array
of settings, we may lure you on an African safari,
to a quaint Welsh village, or an exotic Riviera
location—anywhere and everywhere that adventurous
men and women fall in love.

As publishers of Harlequin Romances, we're
extremely proud of our books. Since 1949,
Harlequin Enterprises has built its publishing
reputation on the solid base of quality and
originality. Our stories are the most popular
paperback romances sold in North America; every
month, six new titles are released and sold at
nearly every book-selling store in Canada and the
United States.

A free catalogue listing all Harlequin Romances
can be yours by writing to the

HARLEQUIN READER SERVICE,
(In the U.S.) 1440 South Priest Drive, Tempe, AZ 85281
(In Canada) Stratford, Ontario, N5A 6W2

We sincerely hope you enjoy reading
this Harlequin Romance.

Yours truly,

THE PUBLISHERS
  Harlequin Romances

Heart
under Siege

by

JOY ST. CLAIR

Harlequin Books

TORONTO • LONDON • LOS ANGELES • AMSTERDAM
SYDNEY • HAMBURG • PARIS • STOCKHOLM • ATHENS • TOKYO

Original hardcover edition published in 1981
by Mills & Boon Limited

ISBN 0-373-02472-X

Harlequin edition published April 1982

Copyright © 1981 by Joy St. Clair.
Philippine copyright 1981. Australian copyright 1981.
Cover illustration copyright © 1982 by Fred Oakley.

All rights reserved. Except for use in any review, the reproduction or utilization
of this work in whole or in part in any form by any electronic, mechanical or
other means, now known or hereafter invented, including xerography,
photocopying and recording, or in any information storage or retrieval system,
is forbidden without the permission of the publisher, Harlequin Enterprises
Limited, 225 Duncan Mill Road, Don Mills, Ontario, Canada M3B 3K9. All the
characters in this book have no existence outside the imagination of the
author and have no relation whatsoever to anyone bearing the same name
or names. They are not even distantly inspired by any individual known
or unknown to the author, and all the incidents are pure invention.

The Harlequin trademark, consisting of the words HARLEQUIN ROMANCE
and the portrayal of a Harlequin, is registered in the United States Patent
Office and in the Canada Trade Marks Office.

Printed in U.S.A.

CHAPTER ONE

WANTED: YOUNG SINGLE COMPANION/
SECRETARY FOR ENGLISH-BORN WOMAN
LIVING IN KENTUCKY, U.S.A. OWN
APARTMENT AND USE OF CADILLAC. APPLY
BOX NO. . . .

Gemma picked up the women's magazine which her
younger sister pushed across the breakfast table and
read the advertisement marked with a pencilled ring.

'Really, Una!' A wry smile dimpled the corners of
Gemma's mouth. 'When I said I would like to get away
I didn't intend leaving the country exactly.'

'This is a heaven-sent opportunity for you to spread
your wings.' Una leaned her arms on the table and tilted
her fair head. 'You can't spend the rest of your life in
this social backwater, watching television every night,
helping mother run the school . . .'

'True!'

'I thought you liked helping me,' protested Mrs
Geary, seated at the head of the table. It was a private
preparatory school founded by her late husband and
very dear to her heart.

'I love it,' said Gemma. 'But it's time for a change.'

'You'd make a marvellous companion,' enthused
Una. 'And Mother will give you a reference for the secretary part, because you practically run the administration side of things.'

'There'll be hundreds of applicants for the job,'
murmured Gemma. 'I wouldn't stand a chance.'

'You won't get it if you don't apply!' Una smiled
dreamily. 'Think of it! Bluegrass, horse farms, the
Kentucky Derby—and use of Cadillac! A whole new

5

ball-game! I could come and visit you . . .'

'Let me get the job first!' Gemma laughed, a soft sweet sound.

'Now don't rush on too fast, Gemma.' Mrs Geary looked at her elder daughter and wondered for the hundredth time how she had produced a girl of such serene beauty. With her high cheekbones and those fascinating eyes, their colour midway between azure and hyacinth-blue, there was no denying that Gemma was something special—even with her long honey-blonde hair dragged back in that unbecoming bun! She hadn't always worn it in that severe style, only since Rowan had died . . . 'Why don't you try for a position in England first? Running halfway across the world seems a bit drastic. What happens if things go wrong? It's nice then to have your family to catch you when you fall.'

'That's just it.' Gemma rose and crossed the warm kitchen to the window to stare out over the orchard where sheep grazed beneath the bare gnarled trees. In the distance the rolling Buckinghamshire countryside was spread out in brown fields, their harrow-tines rigid with frost. 'My family and friends stifle me with their concern for me. I can't face any more matchmaking. I'm sick of foursomes and blind dates. At least in Kentucky people wouldn't feel pity for me and try their darnedest to get me married off.'

Mrs Geary's expression softened. 'Your friends only want to help. After all, Rowan has been dead for over a year now. It's time to start meeting people again.'

'Men, you mean!' said Gemma grimly. 'Can't you understand? I'm a one-man woman.' She fingered the pendant at her throat, a gold Zodiacal scorpion inlaid with jade. 'And Rowan was that man.'

'I know, dear.' Mrs Geary attempted a light smile. 'But you're barely twenty-two and you were only engaged to Rowan . . .'

'Only engaged!' Gemma echoed indignantly. 'It was

the kind of love that comes once in a lifetime.' Oh, they'd had this argument so many times. She and Rowan had known each other since childhood and their love had been deep and pure, for both were romantics. They had been engaged for eighteen months when he was killed on his motorcycle. A dark wet road, a fatal skid, and her future had lain in ruins. If only they'd married instead of getting engaged, she thought wistfully, at least she might have had a child to care for. But Rowan was studying to be a doctor and marriage had seemed out of the question. 'Other men seem insincere and immature after Rowan,' she said, her voice trembling with emotion.

'And don't you let them know it!' said Una. 'The way you put them down with that ice-maiden treatment. Talk about twenty degrees below! You have "keep off" written all over you.'

'I just let them know I'm not interested,' shrugged Gemma evenly. 'Surely that's preferable to leading them on.' She lifted her chin defiantly. 'I *will* apply for that job.'

A month later, Gemma received a letter from a Mr Shade Lambert informing her that she was on the short list of twelve applicants for the job in Kentucky and inviting her to attend an interview in London at four o'clock the following Wednesday.

Mr Lambert ascribed great importance to the requirement that the person who eventually secured the position must be single with no plans for marrying in the foreseeable future.

'That's me,' said Gemma blithely.

'I suppose Shade is short for something,' mused Una, studying the flamboyant signature on the letter. 'Although you never can tell with Americans.'

'He may be an English agent acting for the advertiser,' Gemma pointed out.

'Not with a name like Shade,' insisted Una. She added darkly, 'Whatever nationality he is, he'll be highly devious in his questioning. They use subtle methods in interviews these days, I hear, so watch out how you answer the most innocent of questions.'

On Wednesday morning, Una had a mischievous sparkle in her eyes as she watched Gemma dithering in front of her wardrobe. 'You must wear your sage-green woollen dress. It shows off your tall, willowy frame to perfection. The Yanks are suckers for the English-rose look, and you're a classic example. Cool and collected with a hint of fire burning within! Shade Lambert will fall like a ton of bricks.'

Gemma hid a smile. 'That isn't the object of the exercise. I've got to look efficient.'

'Go on!' grinned Una. 'It won't hurt if he falls for you too.'

'I wish you luck,' said Mrs Geary doubtfully as Gemma prepared to set off. 'You've led a very sheltered life and Rowan protected you from the world. My poor lamb, I have an idea you're about to be thrown to the lions.'

'She knows what she's doing,' Una winked. 'I reckon it was the "use of Cadillac" that clinched it!'

Gemma travelled by train to Baker Street and took a taxi to Piccadilly. It was ages since she'd been to London, for Rowan had been the quiet, country-loving type of man. Staring out at the rain-lashed streets, she experienced a sinking feeling in the pit of her stomach.

Was she cut out for the kind of interview that this promised to be? What ever was she thinking of, planning to give up her well-ordered life in a sleepy village to seek her fortune in that bustling land across the Atlantic?

Her destination was a suite of offices belonging to an export firm on the top floor of an impressive modern block. She passed through a busy typing pool and was greeted by a talkative young secretary who led the way to a small waiting-room.

Yes, the secretary informed her, Mr Lambert was an American gentleman and he was in England for a couple of weeks. He had borrowed this office for the purpose of conducting the interviews and the applicants had been coming and going all day.

'I'm afraid we're running late and you're the last on the list,' the girl added. 'Would you like to join the rest of those waiting?'

Gemma sat down beside three other women and studied the opposition covertly. There was a brunette with the ramrod bearing of an English nanny; a mousey-haired girl who played nervously with the straps of her weighty briefcase; and a stunning redhead, fashionably dressed in a skin-tight white trouser suit. One by one they were called into the office until Gemma was left alone.

She wasn't used to central heating and slipped off her camel jacket, then went to the wide window to gaze out over the lights of London.

At five-thirty the redhead emerged from the office and smiled confidently at Gemma. 'The job's mine, sweetie. You might as well go home.'

The secretary grimaced after the retreating figure in white. 'Fancies herself!'

Gemma put her hand on the ornate knob and opened the door. She found herself in a spacious room where the oak panelled walls and mock fireplace, complete with copper chimney breast, had an immediate dwarfing effect. In the centre was a massive antique desk cluttered with telephones.

Shade Lambert was standing in front of a book-case writing on a notebook which he held in his hand. He did not glance up as she entered. 'Take a seat,' he said in a pleasant Southern drawl. 'I won't keep you a moment.'

She remained standing, the better to study his tall, well-proportioned frame. He was six foot three at least and there was not an ounce of surplus flesh on him. He wore an expensive navy suit and the cuffs of his pale blue shirt were crisp and immaculate, giving him an air of sophistication while emphasising the bronzed skin of his neck and hands, a tan which made Gemma think of holidays in Bermuda. His hair was cut to a fashionable length and the deep waves were so densely black she felt that if she touched them she would stain her hands! He was about thirty, she decided. Although his head was bent she could see that his features were rugged with a slightly aquiline nose and generous mouth.

As he finished writing and looked in Gemma's direction, she noted that his eyes were a clear amber-brown, fringed with sweeping lashes so thick and dark they gave his lower lids a smudged appearance.

He came towards her across the great expanse of carpet. Goodness, he was handsome, she thought, and didn't he know it! Conceit and self-confidence were written in every step he took.

He stopped in his tracks and his eyes raked her from head to toe, so thoroughly she could almost feel their probing impact. It was the frank stare of a man who was conscious of the effect he had upon women and aimed to reduce her to a quivering mass. As the sweep of his eyes took in every curve of her body, her honey-bright hair, blue eyes and softly glowing skin, she was irritated to discover that sex was raising its ugly head even here in the interview room.

Normally she would have brought her withering ice-maiden glance into play, but she felt at a disadvantage. If she were to succeed in getting the job she must create a good impression, not start off on the wrong foot. She smiled thinly, feeling her cheeks growing warm under his bold scrutiny.

'Excuse me one moment,' he murmured, going to the door to speak to the secretary outside.

Gemma took a deep steadying breath and turned her attention to a large picture which dominated the wall above the fireplace. It was a painting of several orchids in full riotous colour, larger than life and far too gaudy for Gemma's taste.

'Miss Geary? I'm sorry to have kept you waiting. I'm Shade Lambert.' He greeted her with a wide smile, displaying whiter-than-white teeth, and grasped her hand firmly. Then inclining his head towards the painting, he remarked, 'What do you make of it?'

She considered it for a moment longer. 'I prefer simpler flowers.'

'Such as?'

Her mind went blank. Rowan had always given her violets. 'Well, gardenias,' she replied cautiously, suddenly on her guard, recalling Una's warning of devious ploys and wondering if the interview had started.

Once again he asked her to be seated, his tone imperious as if he wished the matter completed with all possible speed. Gemma realised that he must be thoroughly sick of the whole business by now.

She took the chair he indicated and, digging a slender heel into the thick pile of the carpet, crossed her long legs.

He moved towards a well-stocked cocktail cabinet in the corner of the room. 'Would you care for a drink, Miss Geary?'

'I'd love a cup of tea,' she declared without thinking. Then, 'But perhaps that's out of the question, so I'll settle for a tonic water.' She needed to keep a clear head.

He dropped into a leather armchair the other side of the desk and pressed an intercom buzzer to order a tray of tea. Then he picked up a gold pen and made a note on a pad. As his hands drew a sheaf of papers from a folder she recognised the pale green sheet on top as her letter of application.

'I liked your letter,' he remarked, drumming his fingers on the desk. 'Your handwriting is open and forthright . . .'

So they'd even analysed the handwriting! Una's forecasts seemed to be gathering credence.

'But this letter of reference is signed by a Mrs Geary.' He gazed narrowly at her. 'A relative?'

'My mother. She runs the school where I work.'

'It's very complimentary. Could she be biased?' He spoke lightly with just a suspicion of underlying sarcasm.

She glanced at him sharply, forcing herself to hold his gaze. She was about to say 'possibly' but changed it to "Undoubtedly!" She had a feeling she was not going to come through this interview very well, so she might as well give as good as she got!

He grinned, completely disarming her, and said, 'The letters from your bank manager and church minister seem to be in order.'

'They've both known me since I was a child . . .' Her words tailed off. He would have gathered that.

He pushed a packet of king-sized cigarettes towards her. 'Help yourself,' he offered.

'No, thanks, I don't.' She watched him make another note. So he *was* filling in such details! Perhaps it would all be fed into a computer later, she reasoned. She noticed there were no stubs in the ashtray and could not resist saying, 'No applicant is going to admit to being a smoker whether it's true or not, Mr Lambert.'

He looked taken aback and ran his hand through his hair. 'I've observed there are no nicotine stains on your fingers, Miss Geary.' Another smile creased his features. 'And your skin is far too clear for you to be a heavy smoker.'

Gemma felt her cheeks flaring again and jerked her

foot agitatedly. Oh, he was too smooth by half!

There came a knock on the door and the secretary entered bearing a silver tray of tea and biscuits which she placed on the desk in front of him. He glanced impatiently at his watch, then frowned at the girl, 'We're running late, honey. Will you cancel my appointment with Blake? Tell him I'll ring him this evening.'

The girl nodded and withdrew.

'Would you care to pour, Miss Geary?' he asked. 'Russian for me, please. That's . . .'

'I know what Russian tea is!' she answered irritably, immediately regretting her impulsive retort. He had probably only intended to be helpful.

He received her reproof in silence, but his eyes glinted dangerously.

She rose and went around the desk to stand beside him. He watched as she poured his tea, black with a slice of lemon, in the translucent bone china cup. She knew that her hands were shaking and was exasperated to see her own milky brew brim over into the saucer as she added three sugar lumps.

'How do you manage to keep your slim figure with such a sweet tooth?' he remarked lightly.

'Do you have to enter that on your list too?' she enquired, raising her brows. 'I'm afraid I don't know the answer.'

He seemed to detect that she was mocking him and shot her a wry glance. 'No, no, I was just passing a remark . . .' His hand went through his hair again and she recognised the nervous habit. So she had succeeded in rattling him, she thought with satisfaction.

He visibly pulled himself together and went on, 'I really am most sorry for keeping you waiting for so long. But I feel obliged to go into these interviews in depth as I'm acting for another.'

'It's quite all right. I understand.' She sat down, crossed her legs again and took a sip from her cup.

'No, you don't understand at all, Miss Geary.'

She looked at him quickly and jerked her foot again.

'Let me explain.' He leaned back in the chair and swivelled it gently. 'I'm a neighbour of Mrs Prescott, the lady who placed the advertisement which you so kindly answered. I was coming to England to look at some horses and I offered to conduct the interviews for her.'

Gemma idly wondered if he owned one of the famous Kentucky horse farms which Una had mentioned.

'The successful applicant will be paid a generous salary, plus her air fare, so you understand I have to get it right.' He steepled his fingertips and went on, 'The job entails running the office for Mrs Prescott and accompanying her to social functions. She is the widow of a tobacco farmer, elderly but in good health, and she employs an adequate staff.' He paused and once again directed a sweeping glance over her face and figure. 'What Mrs Prescott requires is a lively young companion. The fact is, Miss Geary, I've been asked to engage a sensible English girl who's not likely to leave after a few months in order to get married. You see, the American girls who've been employed in the past have had a habit of leaving just when they've learned Mrs Prescott's little idiosyncrasies and she's getting tired of the process . . .'

'I have no intention of getting married!' Gemma cut in firmly. 'You can be quite certain of that.'

'Oh, really?' He looked sceptical and when he spoke again his voice had deepened noticeably. 'How can you be so sure?'

'Because . . .' Oh dear, it wasn't going to be easy to convince this man of her intentions to pursue a career only. She wondered how far she should go in trying to explain her motives. Perhaps it would be smart to get up and leave now.

But he looked so smug, so all-knowing, she felt obliged

to puncture his arrogance. 'Because I have no interest in men whatsoever.'

'Now that's intriguing!' He turned down the corners of his mouth in an exaggerated grimace. 'How come? Let me guess. You've been let down, Miss Geary. Jilted?' He was deliberately baiting her. 'Ah, you're angry with him at the moment and you think you hate all men, but that feeling will pass . . .'

This was really too much, she thought, as her pulses quickened. 'I have not been jilted, Mr Lambert. If it's any of your business, which I very much doubt, I was engaged to a wonderful man who died just over a year ago.'

'Oh, I see. Forgive me.' He stopped swivelling in the chair and leaned his elbows on the desk. 'But I fail to see how that makes you so sure you'll never be interested again.'

'Because I shall never find anyone like him again,' she said raising her voice. This was a well-versed argument and she felt competent to thrash the matter out. 'And I will not take second best.'

He treated her body to another searing glance and this time it was charged with insolence. 'You're a very attractive young woman, Miss Geary. I guess you'll have your work cut out convincing the young men you're serious. It might be hard to resist them.'

'My fiancé was one in a million. I was lucky,' she declared hotly, annoyed with herself, knowing she was rubbing him up the wrong way, but unable to ignore the challenge in his eyes. What a way to conduct an interview! And what a way to try to get a job! It was plain she wouldn't be considered now, so she saw no reason to spare him. The job was of no consequence any more. This was between herself and Mr Lambert. 'As to the average man of today,' she continued disparagingly, 'he's so insincere, so uncouth, that on the contrary I find it very easy to resist his pathetic advances . . .'

He shook his head in disbelief. 'Oh dear, Miss Geary! I can see that the whole of the male population of the world is condemned in your eyes.' His voice underwent a subtle change to become derisive. 'However, you're young, and the time will come when you will forget your fiancé . . .'

She jumped up, a forcible anger mounting inside her until she wanted to hit out at this self-satisfied American with his insulting remarks. How dared he suggest she was mistaken about her feelings! Her fingers went automatically to where the jade pendant nestled against her chest and she was comforted by the feel of the hard metal. 'Never!' she cried, her eyes sparkling with indignation. 'It was the real thing, a once-in-a-lifetime experience which I know could never be repeated.' She held her chin high. 'I see no point in continuing with this interview if you're not prepared to believe one word I say.'

'Miss Geary,' he implored, rising also, 'please remain seated. Forgive me if I sound sceptical, but I've observed human behaviour in all manner of situations and I know . . .'

'You know nothing, Mr Lambert!' She delivered the words contemptuously and walked towards the door. Pausing, she swung round. 'Are you married?'

He shook his head. 'No, I'm not,' he said vehemently. 'I know enough of human nature to be sure that there's no such thing as a once-in-a-lifetime experience.'

Gemma stared pityingly at him. 'I'm sorry for you then.' She placed her hand on the door handle. 'I fail to see how this has anything to do with engaging a companion/secretary, but obviously it has . . .'

'If you'll only come back and sit down, we can discuss the matter sensibly . . .'

'No!' She spat out the word. 'I refuse to be addressed in such a condescending way. Thank you for seeing me,

Mr Lambert. I'm sorry to have taken up so much of your valuable time. You'll be able to keep your appointment with Blake after all.'

She darted into the outer office and grabbed her jacket from the back of the chair. 'What an impossible man!' she said to the startled secretary.

In her anxiety to get away, Gemma struggled with the jacket and was dismayed to find that one of the sleeves was inside out. A moment later she felt the garment being taken from her hands and turned to see Shade Lambert in his rôle as charming interviewer sorting out the sleeve and holding the jacket open for her to put on.

This time her arm missed the sleeve altogether and she dropped her bag on the floor. She could have wept with frustration. After retrieving the bag and snatching the jacket from his astonished hands, she fled from the room.

'We'll be in touch,' called the secretary.

'I doubt it!' muttered Gemma, her face burning as she stormed between the rows of now-empty desks in the typing pool.

She felt herself shaking with anger as she went down in the lift. What a waste of time!

She reached the ground floor before a sense of disappointment overcame her. What had she expected? Dragging her steps dispiritedly, she reproached herself for letting personalities intrude. Heavens, he was hardly her type. Why had she acted so defensively?

Talk about making a fool of herself! Where was the cool ice-maiden now?

There was a bar immediately opposite the block of offices and she crossed to get herself a gin and tonic. She needed something stronger than tea right now.

As she sank thankfully into a leather armchair by the window, she noticed the stunning redhead sitting at a nearby table and nodded cordially to her. However, the greeting went unnoticed, for the other girl was too pre-occupied watching the office block opposite. Gemma recalled the words 'The job's mine, sweetie. You might as well go home'. It was probably true. The redhead was young and lively all right. But how had she managed to convince Mr High-and-Mighty Lambert that she was not interested in marriage?

The drink revived Gemma and she began to get the day's events into perspective. Oh, why had she laid herself open to such a gruelling experience? If this was high-powered commercialism then she wanted none of it. She was content to remain working at the school for ever.

She was draining her glass and thinking about getting back to Baker Street station when she observed the red-head rise to her feet and rush to the door. Gemma glanced across the road and was surprised to see Shade Lambert standing on the pavement opposite.

Gemma watched the redhead dodge the traffic to cross the road. The man and girl greeted each other with a smile. After a few moments' conversation, Shade Lambert hailed a taxi and the two of them got into it.

So he had made a date to see the girl again, mused Gemma, philosophically. That was his type, was it? It was now quite clear who was going to get the job!

A couple of weeks later, Gemma was checking the linen cupboard at the school when Una came running along the corridor waving a white envelope.

'Gemma, this just came. London postmark, same type of envelope as before. It's from Shade Lambert!'

'One of his lackeys, more likely,' grimaced Gemma, 'telling me they're sorry but they've now filled the post.'

'Aren't you going to open it?' asked Una, holding it up to the light.

'Oh, you read it for me,' said Gemma. 'I can see you're dying to. Just tell me the worst.'

Una tore at the envelope and hurriedly scanned the

page of typescript. 'Well, well!' she exclaimed. 'Listen to this. "Mr Shade Lambert has great pleasure in informing you that you have the position of companion/secretary to Mrs Henrietta Prescott, in Lexington, Kentucky. He is returning to America this week, but Mrs Prescott will be in touch".'

'I don't believe it,' said Gemma, snatching the letter away and staring at it. 'How extraordinary!'

Una watched her sister thoughtfully. 'I suppose now you're going to say you won't accept the job, just to be awkward!'

'Oh, no!' Gemma's eyes gleamed maliciously. 'I'm not giving Shade Lambert the satisfaction of thinking I'm not capable after all. And I've got to prove to him that I meant what I said about remaining single!'

'You're a dark horse,' said Una slyly. 'You led us to believe that you didn't stand an earthly. You said that redhead . . .'

'I don't understand it,' Gemma slowly. 'I was really rude to the man. What on earth made him . . .?'

'He was probably more astute than you thought,' said Una, placing her arm about Gemma's shoulders. 'He could see that underneath all your harsh words you were just what they were looking for. He's not such an ignoramus after all. And you'll soon be able to apologise to his face.'

'What do you mean?' asked Gemma, her eyes narrowing.

'Well, you said he was a neighbour of Mrs Prescott, so he's bound to be a regular visitor . . .'

'Hm!' sneered Gemma. 'In Kentucky neighbours live miles apart.'

'Well, you'll be able to hop into the Cadillac and drive over to see him!' said Una with a smile.

The air ticket duly arrived and for the next few weeks Gemma was concerned with obtaining a passport, visa and work permit. The form-filling seemed endless.

Una telephoned the American Embassy and discovered that, although Kentucky was described as a
Southern state, it was known to experience cold weather
in March, so after some last-minute doubts and a tearful
farewell, Gemma set off suitably attired in a strawberry-
pink woollen suit.

She travelled by jumbo jet to New York, then trans-
ferred to a smaller airline. The aircraft landed smoothly
at Lexington airport and Gemma went straight to the
lounge where she had arranged to be met by a member
of Mrs Prescott's staff.

'Hi there! You must be Gemma Geary.'

Gemma was being addressed by a woman in her early
thirties with nutbrown curls, bright button eyes and a
smile which came readily to her unassuming features.

'That's me. And you're . . .?'

'Vikki Norris.' The woman's accent was pure *Gone
with the Wind*. She held out her hand. 'I'm Mrs
Prescott's housekeeper. I sure am pleased to meet you.
You must be worn out. Let's get to the car and take
you home, then you'll be able to grab some sleep this
afternoon.'

Vikki led the way to the parking lot where a gleaming
lilac-coloured Cadillac awaited them, at least twenty feet
long with seating for nine.

A stocky middle-aged chauffeur, smartly clothed in a
slate-grey uniform, slid from the front seat and ground
out his cigarette with the heel of a black boot. Vikki
introduced him as Yarwood.

'Hi!' He casually flicked the peak of his cap before
stowing Gemma's luggage in the roomy trunk.

'So this is the Cadillac!' breathed Gemma. 'I'm impressed.'

The two women climbed into the back seat and sank
down on the soft upholstery. The long sleek vehicle
purred to life to bear them silently and swiftly through

the city and out the other side till presently they were passing through a horse farming area.

Tired as she was, Gemma was enthralled by the sight of miles of whiteboard fencing, elegant farmhouses and efficient-looking horse barns dotted about the vast acres of grassland.

'Aren't there a lot of farms!' she exclaimed.

'Yes, there are supposed to be three hundred and fifty of them around Lexington,' agreed Vikki. 'Some are open to the public, like your country houses in England. Mrs Prescott's home, Clairmond, is in a residential district just beyond the farms.'

'Where's the famous bluegrass of Kentucky?' asked Gemma, peering at the pastures and lawns.

'That's it.'

'But it's green!'

'I'm afraid so.'

They reached a grove of stately trees and the car turned in between high stone pillars. A black gardener waved to them from an ornamental shrub garden as they proceeded along a gravelled drive which circled immaculate lawns. And suddenly there it was—a solid two-storey Georgian mansion of rose-red brick with four gleaming-white Ionic columns. With its steep small-tiled roof, finely moulded cornices and balanced chimneystacks, it was an exercise in symmetry.

'Welcome to Clairmond,' grinned Vikki. 'Mrs Prescott is waiting inside to meet you.'

As Gemma went up the wide steps her heart began to quicken at the prospect of meeting her employer at last. Supposing they were not compatible! Supposing she was not cut out to be a companion! It was a long way to come to find out it was all a ghastly mistake.

A middle-aged maid and two younger women gathered round to sort out the suitcases which Yarwood had set down on the green marble floor of the spacious hall. It was like standing in a cathedral, thought Gemma.

At the far end of the hall there rose a wide staircase which, halfway up, divided into two flights leading in opposite directions.

Although the house was built in the style of old-world elegance, Gemma was to discover that the furniture throughout was contemporary, coupled with the most up-to-date aids to modern living.

Vikki opened a pair of white double doors and ushered Gemma into a drawing-room. 'Just wait there a moment, Mrs Prescott will be along directly.'

Gemma set her handbag down on an onyx occasional table and looked admiringly at the pale green walls and burgundy damask curtaining. She had crossed to the Italian marble mantelpiece to examine some fine silverglass, when she heard the door open again.

'Miss Geary!' The word was not a question but a command.

She swung round to see a very old lady walking towards her with the aid of an ebony stick.

It was an unforgettable moment. Mrs Prescott was a woman who would stand out in any crowd. Taller than average, and well-proportioned, her bearing was quite majestic. Her pure white hair, swept back into a cluster of curls, framed an oval face, heavily made up in an attempt, not wholly successful, to hide the ravages of time, while her black eyes and well-shaped brows gave life and intelligence to her expression. She wore a tangerine trouser suit with cream facings.

'So you're Gemma Geary!' Her voice was low and rasping and very American. 'Turn around and let's have a look at you.'

Speechless, Gemma did as she was told.

'Hm!' said the other, knitting her mouth into a knot and leaning heavily on her stick. 'Shade Lambert didn't say the half of it.'

Gemma gulped and fiddled nervously with the buttons of her suit.

'Got a tongue in your head?' snapped the old woman.

'Yes!' Gemma declared with a dignified toss of her head. 'Yes, I have!' she said more boldly. 'I presume you're Mrs Prescott?'

The old lady stared for a moment, then her thin carefully-drawn lips emitted a laugh. 'That's better!' She thrust out a wrinkled hand. 'Welcome, Gemma Geary.'

Gemma's pent-up breath escaped with a rush of relief and she grasped the hand firmly. 'I'm delighted to meet you.'

'Delighted!' echoed Mrs Prescott, imitating Gemma's accent. 'You don't know what pleasure it gives me to hear your voice. I'm afraid I lost my English accent a long time ago.' She dropped into an armchair and squinted up at Gemma. 'How was the trip?'

'Trouble-free, but tiring,' Gemma replied. 'I suppose I'm suffering from jet-lag.'

Mrs Prescott picked up a brass bell from a nearby table and jangled it impatiently. 'Vikki!' she called. 'Take Miss Geary to her apartment and arrange for some tea.' Looking at Gemma, she said, 'We'll meet again at dinner this evening.'

Vikki led the way up the imposing staircase and along the thickly carpeted corridor.

'Well, what do you think of her?' Vikki watched Gemma's expression closely.

'A very candid lady, I should say.'

'You can say that again,' said Vikki. 'She says exactly what she thinks. You know where you stand with her.' She flung open a door. 'Here we are, then.'

Gemma's apartment consisted of a sitting-room and bedroom, both newly decorated in a colour scheme of pink and cream. A curtained-off recess in the sitting-room contained a small ice box and electric boiling ring—'So you can get a midnight snack if you want to' said Vikki—and leading from the bedroom was a green-tiled bathroom complete with shower.

Gemma's gaze took in the portable television set, the array of jars on the dressing table and the bronze urn filled with yellow roses. 'It's beautiful,' she whispered.

'Glad you like it.'

'Is your room nearby, Vikki?' asked Gemma, appreciative of the other's helpfulness and hoping they could be friends.

'Heavens, no! I don't live in. I'm married.' Vikki went to the door. 'I live in Lexington with my husband and little boy. I work a five-day week here and, believe me, that's enough.' She laughed. 'Don't get me wrong, I love my work, but Mrs Prescott can be a bit of a slave-driver. However, you'll find her bark is worse than her bite. I've asked for a tray of tea to be brought up. Then I suggest you get your head down. Better wear a long dress for dinner. It's at eight.' She jabbed a finger at Gemma and added with mock severity, 'Sharp!'

Gemma went to the window and gazed out to find that her room was at the rear of the house. Immediately below her were three long grassy terraces with broad shrubbed borders descending to a half-moon sliver of still water, while farther away, at the heart of a clump of trees, she saw the glint of gilded tiles which could be the roof of a summerhouse.

She took a leisurely bath, using the expensive essences that had been provided. Then she donned her dressing gown just as the tray of tea arrived. Presently she lay on the soft rose-sprigged duvet convinced she was far too excited to sleep. Yet in a few moments she was lost in dreams and did not wake until the maid knocked on the door with the message that dinner would be served in one hour.

CHAPTER TWO

HOVERING just inside the dining-room door, Gemma saw Mrs Prescott, strikingly attired in pale blue silk with diamonds flashing at her wrists and throat, seated at the head of a splendid glass-topped table which was decked with flowers and flanked by tall ladder-backed chairs.

'Come along in, Gemma,' said the old lady. 'I've invited Shade Lambert to join us for dinner. I hope you'll be pleased . . .' She broke off as the front door bell rang. Half a minute later, Shade stood framed in the doorway.

Those thirty seconds were not long enough for Gemma to prepare herself for the sight of him. She jumped visibly, reminded of their stormy parting in London, and felt her cheeks growing warm.

His eyes immediately went to Gemma and for a moment his gaze flickered over her face like a glancing flame, before he turned his attention to Mrs. Prescott.

'How's my favourite girl-friend?' he asked, bending and dropping a kiss on the wrinkled cheek. 'You look ravishing!'

She beamed up at him. 'You gorgeous man! You're such a flatterer!'

'No flattery at all!' He straightened, then held out his hand to Gemma. 'Ah, Miss Geary,' he said solemnly. 'Glad you made it!'

'Thank you,' she murmured, as his warm fingers closed around hers like steel springs.

He wore a dark-brown lounge suit and beige shirt which did little to disguise the primitive masculinity he radiated. She had forgotten how handsome he was . . . the smudgy lashes, the way those amber eyes could rake her form with such thoroughness!

'I thought that on your first evening here, Gemma, you'd like to see someone you'd already met,' explained Mrs Prescott.

'I'm sure Miss Geary is delighted with your thoughtfulness,' drawled Shade, pulling out a chair for Gemma.

The old lady looked up quickly. 'Do I detect a note of irony in your tone, Shade? Have I done the wrong thing inviting you here tonight?'

'Not at all,' said Gemma politely, sliding into the chair, unnerved by Shade's proximity as he leaned over her, assuring himself she was comfortable.

'Certainly not!' he agreed emphatically, his eyes faintly mocking. His long legs took him behind Mrs Prescott to the seat immediately opposite Gemma. 'Miss Geary and I understand one another perfectly.'

Their hostess frowned. 'There's something going on here that I don't know about,' she grumbled. 'You're not to try any of your tricks on Gemma, Shade. I won't have it!'

He raised his thick brows innocently. 'What tricks are those, Henrietta?'

'You know what I mean,' she replied darkly.

The chicken consommé arrived and Mrs Prescott launched into some reminiscences of her childhood in England. 'Perhaps if Elgiva had been brought up there she wouldn't have turned out so badly,' she concluded.

'Mrs Prescott is referring to her granddaughter,' Shade explained.

'Oh, I didn't know you had a granddaughter,' said Gemma, taking a solid silver knife and fork to the lemon sole which was placed before her.

'I've been her guardian since she was a little girl,' said Mrs Prescott. 'Her father, my only child, was killed in an automobile accident and her mother is living in Argentina with some adventurer or other . . .'

'He's an oilman,' put in Shade. 'Very respectable.'

'Well, whatever he is, they couldn't care less about Elgiva,' declared Mrs Prescott. 'They left me to bring her up.'

'Elgiva is "finishing" in Switzerland,' said Shade, helping Gemma to more of the excellent rosé wine. He smiled intimately, displaying his very white teeth. 'Learning to be a lady.'

'Let's hope they can do something with her,' Mrs Prescott's lips compressed into a peevish line. 'I know I can't.'

'Elgiva's not as bad as Mrs Prescott tries to make out,' argued Shade. 'She's a bit wild, perhaps, but she's young—only eighteen.' He levelled a meaningful gaze at Gemma. 'You know what young women are like thinking they know everything about life—and love!'

Gemma glared at him. She knew very well he was referring to her insistence that she had experienced a once-in-a-lifetime love. She wanted to throw something at his smug countenance and tell him in no uncertain terms that he didn't know what he was talking about. But she was nervous enough as it was on this her first night in America, and didn't feel up to engaging in a verbal battle with him on the subject of personal relationships.

'Bah!' snorted Mrs Prescott, unaware of the turbulent undercurrents passing between her two guests. 'I'm paying good money to that finishing school and I expect them to deliver the goods. She's been gone a year now, so I live in hopes.' She sighed heavily. 'All that young miss thinks about is pop music and clothes.'

'Oh, there's nothing wrong with being fashion-conscious,' protested Gemma.

Mrs Prescott laughed mirthlessly. 'You should see some of the outrageous outfits she collected!' She eyed her new companion shrewdly.

'You'd better get yourself some new clothes, Gemma. We'll make that top priority. You can go into town

with Vikki during the next few days. I shall be giving
you a generous dress allowance.'

'Oh no, I couldn't let you buy my clothes.' Gemma
twisted the stem of her wineglass. 'I'll buy my own.'

'Nonsense!' snapped Mrs Prescott, attacking her lamb
cutlet with vigour. 'You'll be required to attend some
pretty important functions with me. I can't have you
looking like the poor country cousin.'

'Well, thanks,' Gemma felt deflated and selfconsciously smoothed the skirt of her Marks and Spencer
leisure gown—a parting gift from her mother. She had
not worn it before this evening and now she discovered
that the neckline fell open when she leaned forward to
eat, revealing more of her cleavage than she had antici-
pated. Normally it would not have worried her, but she
hadn't expected Shade Lambert to be sitting across the
table from her, ogling her like a schoolboy at a peep-
show.

Shade's mouth twisted wryly and she shot him a hostile
glance. She heard him laugh quietly, an infuriating
chuckle which set her teeth on edge.

'Your dress is delightful, Miss Geary, and you know
it,' he said. 'Don't take too much notice of Mrs Prescott.
She likes to see how far she can go.'

'So I've noticed!' Gemma replied acidly.

Mrs Prescott looked from one to the other of them
and glared, 'Now don't you two go ganging up on me!'

The way she coupled them together, as if they were a
team, sent the colour flooding Gemma's cheeks again.

Shade's eyes dwelt on the delicate contours of
Gemma's face and he said slyly, 'Bossy, isn't she?'

The meal was rounded off with a delicious concoction
of peaches and nectarines in white wine, then Mrs
Prescott lit a Camel cigarette, placed it in a long ivory
holder, and told the maid they would take coffee in the
drawing-room.

They went across the hall and the two women settled

themselves in deep cushioned armchairs while Shade, in response to Mrs Prescott's invitation, selected a classical record and placed it on a complicated-looking quadraphonic music centre. Gemma recognised Bach's Brandenburg Concerto No. 5.

'Yes,' said the old lady, still harping on the subject of Gemma's dress allowance. 'You can drive into Lexington with Vikki in a day or two to get yourself rigged out. No stinting, mind!'

'Any instructions as to the style I'm to purchase?' Gemma asked wickedly.

Mrs Prescott's eyes narrowed momentarily then she gave a delighted chuckle. 'I leave it entirely to you. The English have such good dress sense.' She leaned her head back against her chair and watched a smoke ring ascend to the finely moulded ceiling. 'I love the English!'

'Hm, me too!' Shade muttered almost under his breath.

'What's that?' demanded Mrs Prescott. 'Speak up, for goodness sake!'

Shade's eyes were riveted on Gemma's face. 'I was merely agreeing with you about the lovable qualities of the English race.'

Gemma pressed her lips together. She could have screamed at the way he was flirting with her under Mrs Prescott's very nose.

The old lady ignored the interruption. 'I have a priceless collection of English Georgian silver upstairs. It's kept under lock and key, but Vikki will show it to you, if you're interested. I still consider myself English, although I've lived here for nearly sixty years and I'm a naturalised American citizen.'

Gemma picked up her Sèvres coffee cup with its exquisite design of saffron-yellow shepherdesses on blue enamel, and took a sip. 'Did you ever think of returning to England to live after your husband died?' she asked.

Mrs Prescott kicked off her unsuitable stiletto-heeled shoes. 'I thought of it. I even went as far as taking a trip there. But everything had changed and all the people I'd known had died.' She sighed. 'My family and friends were here, so I stayed.'

Gemma brought a little footstool to put under her employer's feet.

'Thank you,' smiled Mrs Prescott. 'I think you're going to suit me fine, Gemma. Shade, you're a genius!'

Gemma, returning to her chair, noted the smug expression on Shade's face and hastily looked away.

The record reached the exhilarating harpsichord solo and the conversation was abated. Gemma risked a glance at Shade as he stood by the fireplace, lost in thought. Heavens, she thought, he was only a man! Why was she getting so uptight? All his manoeuvres were merely male ploys—sophisticated ploys but ploys nevertheless—to put her in her place as the female sexual object. A cool head was all she needed to handle him. Her sense of proportion came back in a rush and she began to relax at last.

'I'd like to be left alone now,' said Mrs Prescott suddenly.

'Oh!' Gemma faltered. 'I thought perhaps you might like to discuss what my duties will be. We seem to have talked about everything else but what I'm supposed to do.'

'Tomorrow,' said Mrs. Prescott, closing her eyes. 'Vikki will show you everything tomorrow. I'm tired now. Goodnight.'

Shade silenced the record player, dropped a kiss on the old lady's forehead and followed Gemma into the hall, closing the double doors quietly but firmly after him.

Gemma was unable to believe she had been dismissed so abruptly, and her expression must have made this evident.

'Don't be hurt by Mrs Prescott's seemingly callous behaviour.' said Shade. 'She's very old and tries to do too much, then suddenly finds the going too tough and drops out like a light.'

'I see.' Gemma's recent thoughts about him had lulled her into a false sense of security, and she was slightly disconcerted, therefore, when he placed a finger on her forearm and ruffled the tiny pale hairs. She shied away from him and tried to keep her voice steady. 'How old is she?'

'No one dares ask.'

'She's quite fantastic, isn't she?'

'Keeping up appearances, you mean?' he enquired, moving his hand to grip her elbow. 'Well, all American women do that.'

There was no denying that his presence bothered her and she wondered how she was going to excuse herself. She looked up at him breathlessly. 'Well, I'll say good-night ...'

He regarded her from half-closed eyes. 'Things are looking up at Clairmond since I took a hand at choosing companions. The previous ones have been frightful—bright young things with an eye to the main chance.'

Slightly taken aback by his glance, Gemma asked, 'Why doesn't she employ an older person?'

'Because she likes young people around her. She figures they help her stay young.' He turned to face her and his hands fastened upon her waist. 'As I told you, the only thing wrong with that is they've inclined to leave to get married.'

Her heart was experiencing severe palpitations, but she held herself still, reasoning that struggling with him would clearly get her nowhere. 'And as I told you, that won't happen to me ...'

'Because you're not interested in men,' he finished.

She knew he was goading her into another argument, but could not resist rising to the bait. 'Exactly!'

'Still peddling that old line?'

His hands moved from her waist to her shoulders, glancing her breasts on the way. By accident or design, she would never know. One of the tricks Mrs Prescott had alluded to, no doubt. It was only a fleeting touch, but it sent a stream of wariness trickling through her consciousness and her body shook with emotion.

He watched her closely and a leaping flame lit his eyes. 'Why, I can feel you tremble, Gemma.'

'How arrogant you are!' she snapped. 'If I tremble it's because I'm annoyed with you, not because I've fallen under your spell.'

'Annoyed with me?' he lifted one dark eyebrow.

'Yes—it's unbelievable, isn't it?'

'But why?'

'Because you won't take me seriously when I tell you I have no intention of getting involved . . .'

'Suppose I kiss all this nonsense away?' he said suddenly, his voice deep and vibrant. 'Would you still stare at me so defiantly, I wonder?'

For long moments she thought she hadn't heard him properly. There was a long silence during which she felt his grip tighten on her shoulders, then a fount of hysteria rose within her and she laughed nervously. 'You wouldn't dare!'

'No?'

Alarm bells were ringing in her brain and she twisted and turned to be free of him. Just another man, eh? She needed more than a cool head to get out of this situation! She glanced in desperation at the drawing-room, willing Mrs Prescott to come out and break up the party.

'No chance!' he said, following her gaze and practically reading her mind. 'She'll be dreaming by now.'

'Let me go!' Gemma cried. She pushed against his hard chest, but he was immovable.

His mouth swooped towards hers and she quavered

in anticipation and dread. He held her in an unbreakable grip and she knew she must endure his unwanted attentions because she was his prisoner. But just wait till he had finished with her! She would have great pleasure in slapping his hateful face!

He was so close that she felt his warm breath on her lips, then he thrust her away from him and she heard him laugh.

'No, that would be too easy.'

'Oh!' she exclaimed in shocked surprise. 'You . . . you . . .!' She raised her hand to slap him, but he caught it deftly and held it to her side.

She jerked away from him and, summoning all her dignity, began to climb the stairs. 'Leave me alone! You're impossible!'

'Because I didn't kiss you after all?' Shade enquired with infuriating calm. 'That can easily be remedied.'

Her derisive laugh died on her lips as she saw him bound up the stairs two at a time. She turned and fled. She had reached the division of the main staircase when he seized her arm and swung her round to face him. A moment later his hands had spanned her waist.

She was conscious of each one of his fingers. They seemed to burn her flesh through the thickness of her clothes. Did he really mean to kiss her this time? 'Stop playing games with me!' she said icily.

'Kissing games can be quite delightful, Gemma,' he said.

'You speak as an expert, of course!'

'Why, yes! Don't you want to play? Or have you forgotten how?'

She tried to pull away. 'I'll scream!' she warned him, knowing her throat was too dry for her to do anything of the sort.

'I'm sure you wouldn't do anything so childish,' he observed drily. 'Why not wait and see before you give way to panic? You might enjoy it.'

'My God, how conceited you are!' she declared, turning her head as his face drew near to fill her line of vision.

Shade gripped her chin and forced her head round. 'Hang on, Gemma,' he said huskily, 'for the kiss of your sweet young life.'

She held herself rigid. Let him do his worst! she thought. She was determined he would get no satisfaction from kissing this ice-maiden. She screwed up her eyes to blot out his features as his lips descended upon hers.

Clenching her fists, she desperately fixed her mind on the details of the recent meal, anything to stop herself thinking about the onslaught of his kiss. Her stomach was churning in an unfamiliar way and her heart was beating out a military tattoo, but somehow she managed to keep her lips straight, her body arched away from his. She mustn't respond! She mustn't . . .!

It was as if she had built a wall between them, but she was aware that it was made of clay and crumbling fast. She could not keep up this charade much longer. Oh, would the relentless pressure never cease?

All at once her ordeal was over. Shade almost flung her away from him. 'I've never kissed a marble statue before!' he said in disgust.

She gave a brittle laugh. She had succeeded in frustrating him, she thought triumphantly, and her spirits soared. 'What did you expect? Total surrender?'

He looked dazed. He obviously wasn't used to that kind of reaction from his women.

'Now will you leave me alone?' she asked.

Still he stared in disbelief.

She moved in for the kill. 'I'm quite certain it's not part of my duties to satisfy your male ego, Mr Lambert.'

His features relaxed and he shrugged philosophically. When he spoke, all the old arrogance was back. 'There's plenty of time, Miss Geary.'

'I hope you're not going to make a habit of calling round and forcing your attentions on me in this fashion,' she said haughtily before, to her dismay, a great tremulous sigh escaped her. 'Don't you know when you're beaten?' she went on shakily.

He watched her suspiciously, gnawing on his thumbnail. Her involuntary sigh and change of tone appeared to have enlightened him as to the strength of purpose she had employed in resisting him, and he advanced towards her again.

'I don't know that I am beaten,' he said evenly. 'Could you keep up that performance a second time?'

His laugh floated up to her as she raced up the remaining stairs to her apartment. She was shaking with emotion as she entered her sitting-room and threw the bolt on the door. How dared he! Well, she had let him know she had no interest in him whatsoever. She couldn't have made it clearer had she cabled him Western Union. He would have to be very arrogant indeed not to get the message.

Presently she went to her writing desk to pen a letter home. She had so much to tell her mother and sister, but it would need careful editing in case Una got the wrong idea.

'I've been answering most of the letters since the last secretary left,' said Vikki, showing Gemma into the small office the following morning. 'I found it an awful chore because I don't do shorthand and my typing is of the one-finger variety. I take it you're proficient in both subjects?'

'Oh yes,' said Gemma, looking at the desk piled high with unopened mail. The office was situated at the side of the house on the ground floor with a view of a walled courtyard where several vehicles were parked.

'The greatest part of the job is answering the mail

concerning Mrs Prescott's attendances at the various functions,' went on Vikki, pulling open the top drawer of one of the filing cabinets. 'She's on the committee of dozens of charities and likes to support them. All the details are in here and are listed alphabetically, so it should be easy to follow for someone used to office routine. She was a lot more active when she was younger, but these days things have quietened down a good deal.'

Gemma dropped into the black leather swing chair behind the desk and placed her fingers on the keyboard of the electric typewriter. 'She sounds a very caring person.'

'She is.' Vikki perched on the low windowsill. 'You'll have to see me quite often—I shall need to order the supplies of food and linen through you. You're going to be pretty busy. There's a banquet coming up in Frankfort soon, and Mrs Prescott is letting the local schoolchildren use her grounds for their pageant in May. Then you'll be flying up in the private plane to the cottage in Buffalo at Whitsun. I hope you can play bridge. They seem to do nothing else in Buffalo.'

'Yes, I can, but please stop! You're making me dizzy.'

'You'll have to make up the wage packets too,' continued Vikki. 'We're a happy crowd. Besides you and me, there are six hired hands. The maid, Mildred, and Yarwood, the chauffeur, are a married couple and live in over the garage. The rest—cook, gardener and two cleaning women—all live out in Lexington. The parking space alongside this window is usually filled with cars belonging to the staff. Do you drive?'

'Yes, I do, but I'm not too sure about driving on the wrong side of the road . . .' Gemma broke off with embarrassment. 'Sorry, that sounded rude. I meant the *right* side of the road.' She smiled. 'I've got my international driving licence and my sister had visions of me driving the Cadillac. We didn't realise there'd be a chauffeur.'

'You will get the chance to drive it, if you want to,' said Vikki. 'Yarwood will teach you any time you like. He's the pilot too, by the way, if you have a yen to learn to fly . . .'

Gemma held up her hands in mock alarm. 'Please, you're going too fast for me!'

'Well, I'll leave you to get acquainted with the filing system. Let me know if there's anything you don't understand. I'll be in the kitchen.' Vikki paused at the door. 'I have a feeling you're going to fit in very well. Shade Lambert certainly knows his stuff when engaging staff.'

At the mention of Shade Lambert's name, Gemma was irritated to feel her cheeks growing warm. She hastily rummaged through the letters on the desk. 'Does he live near?' she asked as casually as she could.

'He lives with his widowed mother about three miles along the highway,' replied Vikki. 'He owns a horse farm called Five Oaks, considered to be one of the finest in the vicinity. He and Mrs Prescott are as thick as thieves because he can trace his ancestry back to the early English settlers, and that always goes a long way with her.' She clasped her hands together. 'He's a beautiful specimen of manhood, isn't he?'

'I really hadn't noticed,' shrugged Gemma. It was about the biggest lie she had ever uttered!

Vikki glanced sharply at Gemma's flushed cheeks. 'Still, they do say he breaks hearts as often as other men change their socks!'

Gemma spent the rest of the day taking dictation from Mrs Prescott, typing letters, familiarising herself with the dictaphone and rearranging the filing system how she liked it, with a short break for lunch.

At four o'clock a tray of tea was brought in to her and she stood at the window, cup in hand, her cardigan draped about her shoulders, to observe that rain was falling. She noticed that there was now a mud-spattered Range Rover parked in the courtyard and wondered idly if Mrs Prescott had a visitor.

All at once there came a sharp rap on the door and it opened to reveal Shade Lambert standing there eyeing her quizzically.

'Hi!'

The colour rushed to her cheeks and she swung round to rattle the cup into the saucer as her cardigan slid to the floor. In a flash he had bent to retrieve the garment, shaking it out with the obvious intention of replacing it about her shoulders, but she took it from his grasp and threw it on to the chair.

He sighed with exasperation. 'One of these days I'll succeed in helping you on with your jacket!' He seized her hand and shook it firmly.

Gemma regarded him resentfully. There was an air of sensuality about him that was vaguely disturbing. His sheepskin coat and light-coloured drill trousers seemed to enhance his raw masculinity and his damp hair and cold hand indicated that he had come in search of her the moment he had arrived at the house.

His frankly admiring glance swept leisurely over her smooth apricot jumper and slim black skirt, and she experienced an unexpected sensation of satisfaction. Her reaction surprised her. She usually countered such looks with glacial aloofness. Help, she was going to pieces!

She recalled the way he had behaved the previous evening, threatening to kiss her, thrusting her away, then carrying out the threat. She hoped he wasn't going to refer to the matter.

His thickly-lashed eyes moved to the neat pile of stamped envelopes lying on the desk. 'You've wasted no time getting down to work,' he observed with surprise.

'I'm a working girl, Mr Lambert.' She found her voice at last and added sternly, 'I must earn my salary.'

'Relax,' he replied easily, sitting on the edge of the

desk and crossing his ankles. 'Don't be so much on the defensive every time someone makes an innocent remark. You don't have to prove yourself to me.'

· His pose exuded self-confidence and instinct warned her anew that here was a man to be reckoned with.

'You particularly!' she corrected him haughtily.

Shade threw back his head and laughed, a deep throaty sound that echoed around the tiny room. 'But I chose you.'

Flustered, she began to tuck in the wayward strands of her pale hair.

His indolent gaze followed her fingers. 'Why do you wear your hair in such an unbecoming style?'

'Unbecoming?' she asked hotly.

'No, that's the wrong word,' he drawled. 'The style doesn't detract from your beauty one iota. Severe is the word.'

'My hairstyle is none of your business!' She picked up the filing box. 'Now, if you don't mind, I have work to do.'

He was not to be sidetracked. 'Is it to put prospective men friends off?'

'Would you kindly go away?' she snapped. 'I'm paid to work . . .'

He took the box from her nervous fingers and replaced it on the desk. 'So that they'll leave you alone to remain faithful to your dead sweetheart without too much effort?' he continued relentlessly.

Gemma flinched at the intended sarcasm. 'How dare you? I don't need severe hairstyles to help me remain faithful to Rowan.'

'But it sure helps if you're not tempted, eh?' He arched his dark expressive brows.

She felt her anger simmering but forced a contemptuous laugh. 'Oh, I'm not tempted!'

Shade's eyes became two insolent pinpoints. 'You're not succeeding, you know.'

She met his look coldly. 'Now what are you talking about?'

A sardonic smile creased his features. 'You're not succeeding in putting men off. You just present them with a challenge.'

'So, in effect, I'm really leading them on?' she asked incredulously. 'Your logic is quite overwhelming, Mr Lambert.'

'Call me Shade.'

'Mr Lambert!' She fingered the jade pendant nestling against her chest. 'I wear my hair this way because it's manageable. And I shall continue to do so for as long as it pleases me.'

He stared at the pendant. 'Your fiancé gave you that, did he? This Rowan of whom you speak. You seem to derive comfort from touching the thing. Isn't it rather cold and impersonal? An object with no warmth?'

'It's warm all the time it's next to my body,' she answered triumphantly.

He grimaced goodhumouredly. 'I stand corrected.'

'Look,' she said with a sigh, 'if there are so many things wrong with me, why did you choose me to be Mrs Prescott's companion? You were given carte blanche to choose whoever you liked.'

For long moments his pensive eyes studied the planes of her face. 'You were the only one who dared to answer me back.'

She gasped. So that was it!

He pushed himself away from the desk and thrust his hands into the deep pockets of his coat. 'It was no good my engaging a yes-girl. Mrs Prescott is a lively old lady and I had to find someone who would be able to stand up to her, someone who could keep up her end of the argument without losing her cool.'

Gemma lowered her eyes and smiled wryly. 'But I did lose my cool. Remember?'

He laughed again. 'So you did! And very refreshing it was too.'

Gemma dropped into the chair, completely non-plussed. 'I was sure I hadn't got the job,' she murmured, half to herself. 'Especially when I saw you getting into the taxi with that red ...' She broke off and a blush dyed her cheeks again.

'I see!' He eyed her perceptively. 'Jealous?'

'Huh!'

'As a matter of fact, her father had a horse she thought I might be interested in.'

'Don't bother to explain,' she said scathingly, admiring his ingenuity for inventing such a plausible excuse on the spur of the moment. 'It's none of my business what you get up to.'

His smile was infuriating. 'Your lips say that, but your eyes say something else.'

She jumped to her feet and walked around the desk. 'You're boring me, Mr Lambert,' she said, with as much indifference as she could muster. 'Kindly leave.'

He shrugged and appeared about to comply with her request, then suddenly changed his mind and took a step forward. 'We have some unfinished business to attend to—namely, that second kiss.'

Gemma's heart sank. He hadn't got the message at all. 'Keep away from me!' she shouted.

'Scared? So you *were* bluffing!'

With superhuman effort she pushed him out of the way and seized the door handle. 'You seem determined to force yourself upon me!' she cried. 'Won't you be satisfied until you have raped me?'

'When I make love to you, Miss Geary, it won't be rape,' he drawled. 'It will be because you begged me to do it!'

She laughed wildly and wrenched open the door. 'Don't hold your breath, Mr Lambert!' She marched out of the room, head high with pride.

The proverbial fall came swiftly. She caught her foot in the leg of a trolley positioned to the side of the door and, to her chagrin, went sprawling on the hall carpet.

At once Shade was on one knee beside her, rolling her over to a sitting position. 'Have you dented anything?' He sounded amused.

'No, I haven't!' Apart from her dignity, she thought.

Instead of helping her up, as she expected, he cupped her face in his hands and, taking an unfair advantage of her, began to smother her with kisses. His lips began their tantalising trail across her forehead, over her eyelids and down her cheeks, until she was a limp quivering mass of nerves. She knew her mouth was the next port of call and was aware she would never be able to fight him off, lying there in that unrefined position, feeling such a utter fool . . .

'Gemma!' Mrs Prescott's voice came from just around the corner.

Oh no! thought Gemma. To be caught rolling about on the floor with this impossible man!

Shade gathered her into his arms and brought his mouth down squarely on hers, kissing her with such a hungry passion she was forced to yield.

'Gemma, what's happening?' Mrs Prescott's voice was alarmingly close. Any moment she would see them.

Shade got to his feet and, taking Gemma's hand, yanked her to a standing position as easily as if she were a bag of washing.

'I heard voices raised in anger.'

Mrs Prescott hastened around the corner as fast as her stick would allow. As she saw Shade a look of understanding crossed her features. 'Oh, it's you. I might have known!'

Shade touched the old lady's arm and kissed her cheek. 'Just a little experiment I'm conducting, Henrietta, my dear.'

'Now look here,' said Mrs Prescott suspiciously. 'I

don't want any young men enticing my new companion away.'

Shade's lips quirked into a smile. 'You might have your work cut out. She's a very attractive female.'

'Ah, but you're okay, Shade,' went on Mrs Prescott. 'I know you're not the marrying kind. More like the love-'em-and-leave-'em kind. On the other hand, I don't want my new companion's heart broken either.'

Gemma hovered in the corridor, bristling with fury and objecting to being spoken about as if she weren't present. 'There's no fear of that,' she snapped, eyeing Shade with glaring animosity.

He chuckled, completely undaunted. 'Tell you what, Gemma, let's call a truce.'

She stared at him wide-eyed. 'Do you mean that?'

'Sure. There's no reason why we have to fight every time we meet, is there?'

'Are you proposing a platonic friendship between us?' she enquired, staring in amazement. 'That's rich!'

'Stop it, you two!' put in Mrs Prescott.

'Friends, Gemma?' asked Shade.

She took a deep breath. 'All right.'

'You can start by calling me Shade.'

'All right,' she said again, 'Shade.'

'Well, thank goodness that's settled.' Mrs Prescott pouted like a child. 'I'm really put out to find why you came to see Gemma before you came to see me, Shade. I thought I was your number one girl-friend.'

He put his arm about her. 'You certainly are, Henrietta dear.'

Gemma smiled thinly. The man was too smooth by half!

She had reached the stairs before the delayed action from his kisses struck her. Her face still tingled from their blistering impact. She grabbed the newel post for support as her legs turned to jelly. It was then she noticed the ladders which snagged her tights.

Good lord! she thought. If she had to go through that every time he called round . . . It didn't bear thinking about . . .

CHAPTER THREE

GEMMA and Vikki spent the whole of the following day touring the most exclusive dress shops in down town Lexington.

'My favourite occupation!' declared Vikki rapturously. 'Beats housekeeping any day.'

It was amazing, reflected Gemma, how the very mention of Mrs Prescott's name secured for them the utmost attention. They were ushered into the inner sanctums of high fashion, to be brought cups of coffee and fussed over like visiting film stars.

The price tags took Gemma's breath away. 'Oh, I can't,' she moaned time and again. 'It's far too expensive.'

'Stop looking at the tags if they upset you,' advised Vikki. 'Just enjoy yourself with all these magnificent materials.'

'But I feel awful, running up such large bills,' wailed Gemma. 'Can't we go somewhere cheaper?'

'Mrs Prescott will be mad if you don't do as you're told,' scolded Vikki. 'Look on the clothes as a uniform. Just look at that dreamy nightdress,' she murmured as they waited for the latest batch of purchases to be wrapped. She went over to the stand and fingered the silky white garment with narrow shoulder straps and a deep hem of exquisite lace. 'I'll ask the assistant to get it down.'

'No way does that come under the heading of uniform,' said Gemma drolly. 'I mean, who's going to see it?'

'You never know!' giggled Vikki. 'Do have it. You could pay for it yourself if your conscience won't allow you to charge it to Mrs Prescott.' She seized Gemma's arm eagerly. 'Yes, buy it for your trip to the cottage in Buffalo.'

'It is lovely,' murmured Gemma slowly, eyeing the garment covetously. 'I think I will.'

They rounded off the day at the furriers to hunt for a jacket and stole. Vikki rushed Gemma past racks of luxurious coats, towards the back of the shop. 'I'm afraid you won't be allowed to buy anything made from real animal skins,' she explained dolefully. 'Mrs Prescott has strong views about such things. It would be dreadful it you turned up at one of her anti-vivisection meetings wearing a mink. She herself wears only the finest imitations.' She brightened as the assistant appeared with beautiful samples of imitation silver fox and leopard. 'Still, this shop is known for its superb simulated furs, and you honestly can't tell the difference.'

'I'm relieved,' said Gemma. 'I'll be only too happy to purchase something of the cheaper variety.' She idly glanced at the price-tag and gasped. 'But this is almost as expensive as the real thing!'

'I know!' grinned Vikki. 'Isn't it super!'

The veiled sun was low in the sky when they returned to the parking lot for the last time. Yarwood relieved them of their parcels and stowed them in the trunk of the Cadillac.

'Phew! Let's go and have a coffee,' suggested Vikki, pointing to a stall by the entrance to the parking lot.

The three of them were standing drinking from plastic cups when Vikki said suddenly, 'Why, look, here comes Shade Lambert! Seems like he's been doing the same as us.'

Gemma followed the other girl's gaze and saw Shade striding towards them carrying a large store-wrapped parcel under each arm. He wore a white F.B.I.-style raincoat with the collar turned up and carried his car keys in his hand.

He nodded cordially to Vikki and Yarwood then

looked directly at Gemma. 'What are you doing here?'

She wanted to tell him to mind his own business, but she said, 'We're spending Mrs Prescott's money.'

'Ah, the dress allowance!' He treated her to one of his scorching glances. 'I hope I get to see the results of this spending spree.'

'I don't think that's very likely . . .' she began, seething inwardly.

'Gemma!' he chided her gently. 'I thought we called a truce!'

She knew Vikki and Yarwood were watching with interest and forced a smile to her mouth. 'I'm sorry,' she said, flustered, 'but you started it.'

'I started it! How did I do that?' He looked completely baffled.

Her control snapped. 'Making suggestive remarks and looking at me in that way . . . flirting with me while waving a flag of truce! Where's that platonic friendship you promised?'

'Am I flirting with you? Gee, I'm sorry.' He was trying hard to keep a straight face. 'As for the rest, I can't help how I look at you.'

That was probably true, she thought. It was a dyed-in-the-wool habit from way back!

She bit her lip, loath to continue sparring with him here in the street.

Shade gave one of those infuriating laughs guaranteed to set her nerves jangling.

She wished she'd kept her mouth shut now. Hadn't she learned that it was no good trying to have the last word with him? Overcome with embarrassment, she tilted her head to read the store name on one of his parcels. 'Jennifer Jardine—Gowns of Distinction,' she said, raising her eyebrows in an unspoken question.

Before he could say anything they heard the sound of a car horn being honked furiously twenty yards away in the parking lot. As they turned to locate the noise,

Gemma saw a young girl—a vivacious brunette—open the door of a silver-grey Chevrolet and heard her call out, 'Come on, Shade! What's keeping you, honey?'

'Guess that answers your question,' grinned Shade. 'Don't get jealous. She's my cousin.'

Gemma laughed derisively. 'Nice try!'

The girl called out again and Shade said, 'Well, I must go. So long, folks.'

They watched him toss the parcels into the back of the car, then join the brunette in the front seat and take the wheel. Moments later they had driven away.

'Well, well!' said Vikki. 'You and he don't exactly hit it off, do you?'

'I detest the man!' Gemma replied hotly.

'Hm!' Vikki watched Gemma pensively. 'Do you!'

'Now don't *you* start,' said Gemma darkly. 'Having him think I find him irresistible is quite enough.' She paused. 'Who was the brunette?'

'Never seen her before, have you, Yarwood?' asked Vikki.

The man shook his head.

'Still, he's usually got some female in tow,' said Vikki. 'I always think of him as the "big bad wolf". Well, it looks like he has his dinner for tonight!'

When they arrived at Clairmond, Mrs Prescott insisted on inspecting all the garments and nodded with satisfaction. 'You've done well, Gemma. Your taste is impeccable.'

A few days later Gemma had her first taste of her rôle as companion when she accompanied Mrs Prescott to the theatre for a show for the benefit of local nurses.

Gemma wore her new long gown of floral-patterned chiffon over pink shantung. It had a modest neckline and the filmy sleeves were gathered at the wrists. She completed the outfit with gold evening sandals and bag.

The two women were accompanied by an old friend

of Mrs Prescott's, Judge Bradley Dean, who reminded Gemma of an elder statesman with his thick grey hair, rimless spectacles and large cigar.

They arrived at the theatre to be greeted by the cast lined up in the foyer where Mrs Prescott was presented with a bunch of flowers by a little girl. Why, it was almost like a royal premiere, thought Gemma, with Mrs Prescott acting the part of the Queen. The old lady did indeed look regal in a black and silver gown with a small tiara glittering in her hair.

They were taken to a box where Mrs Prescott presented Gemma with some expensive-looking chocolates. The judge took it upon himself to point out to Gemma other well-known local dignitaries and explain the intricacies of the plot of the show. It was a musical based on old Kentuckian folk legends and appeared complicated to a foreigner because it leaned heavily on supernatural goings-on.

When the lights went up for the interval, they made their way to the theatre bar, and it was then that Gemma caught sight of Shade Lambert the other side of the crowded room.

He looked magnificent and manly in a ruffled silk dress shirt, blue cummerbund and black tuxedo. His eyes swept over the gathering and Gemma waited for them to alight upon her, ready to acknowledge him with a curt nod. Then she noticed that he was with the same vivacious brunette for whom he had been carrying the parcels the other day. She wore a low-cut gown of bright scarlet and clung to Shade's arm in a most possessive way.

Immediately Gemma looked away, embarrassed, not wishing to meet his searching gaze. Yet she could not resist another glance, and this time their eyes met.

For a long moment he stared at her, a look of supreme arrogance emanating from his countenance, then he bent his head in a nod of greeting and the ghost of a smile touched his lips.

Confused, Gemma smiled briefly, then turned her back on him.

'Are you enjoying the show?' asked Judge Dean, placing a glass of white wine in her hand.

'What I've understood,' she answered. Her pulses had quickened noticeably and she was aware that her hand shook.

The judge's shrewd old eyes studied her for a moment then he stared across the room at Shade and his companion.

'Mr Lambert seems to have a strange effect on you women,' he observed drily.

Mrs Prescott asked Gemma to accompany her to the ladies' powder-room to give assistance in re-settling the tiara which had become dislodged during the rush to the bar. As Gemma worked with the pins, she wondered if Shade and the brunette had a special understanding. Or was she just a casual acquaintance like the redhead in London?

When they returned to the box Gemma scanned the audience with her opera glasses. She eventually picked out Shade in the third row of the stalls. The girl had leaned her dark hand on his shoulder and he appeared to be whispering to her.

Cousins indeed!

The weather became pleasantly warm and Gemma decided on a long walk in the country. She was feeling sluggish after all those chocolates the other night and the American custom of going in for such large helpings of everything. And she was not used to riding everywhere in cars. If she was not careful she would be putting on weight.

There were wide verges beside the road—for the convenience of horse riders, she had no doubt, for she met no other pedestrians. She started out in the direction of

Lexington and took the first turning she reached. She swung along briskly until she felt her cheeks glowing as her lungs were filled with the fresh clean air.

Several cars passed her, the occupants staring curiously. A couple of them stopped to ask her if she had run out of gas, and offered to help, so unaccustomed were they to seeing a solitary walker.

After an hour she rested, leaning against the white fencing of a farm. Half a dozen yearling horses came to investigate the stranger, hanging their heads over the bars, and she stroked their velvet muzzles. She had an apple in her pocket and, by carefully biting pieces off, she managed to divide it equally between them.

She must have walked three miles, she reckoned and wondered if she had overdone things, acknowledging that she had the same distance to walk back. There was nothing for it but to turn round and start for home.

All at once she saw a rider on a jet black stallion cantering along the border of the field and she paused to watch the graceful pair. Then she recognised Shade Lambert. This must be his farm, she thought. She quickened her pace so as not to be seen. The last thing she wanted was for him to think she had deliberately come in search of him. He was conceited enough already.

He reined in his horse, studied her for a moment, then hailed her before urging his horse over the grassland to jump the fence, mount and rider clearing the obstacle with accomplished ease.

'Gemma Geary!' He spoke in a low amused drawl. 'What are you doing prowling about on your own?'

She squinted up at him. 'Why is everyone so startled to find someone taking a walk?' she asked with chilling aloofness.

He grinned and pushed his fingers through his dense black hair. 'It's not done, you know.'

'By me it is!' she flashed defensively.

Shade dismounted and caught the horse's reins in his

hand, staring at her in that openly sexual way that seemed to be his trademark. He towered above her, the epitome of masculine strength in his white turtleneck sweater and riding breeches. Gemma understood the effect he must have on many women and her own stomach churned with a throb of excitement.

'You look all in. Whatever possessed you to walk so far?'

'I'm perfectly all right,' she snapped. She saw that his tawny eyes called her a liar and she felt bound to qualify the point. 'I walk miles every day in England,' she glowered furiously. How was it that whenever they met he seemed to touch on a raw nerve?

'But you're out of practice.' He regarded her thoughtfully. 'My place is a few hundred yards away. Why don't you come back with me and I'll drive you over to Clairmond?'

'No, thanks.' She was sorely tempted, but hated to admit he was right. 'I'm not a bit tired.'

'Oh, come on.' He took her elbow. 'Admit you've had enough for one day.'

Gemma stared along the deserted road stretching away from her between the fences, and shrugged. 'Well, perhaps I will accept your offer. Mrs Prescott might wonder where I am ...' It sounded so lame she wished she'd kept silent.

Shade grinned sardonically, seeing right through her. He fell into step beside her, leading the horse with one hand and placing the other on the small of her back. 'It's one thing being independent, another being plain stubborn.'

'All right, don't keep on,' she said impatiently, alarmed by the feel of his hand. She endeavoured to quicken her step to be free of him, but he lengthened his stride to keep pace with her.

She glanced surreptitiously at his profile. Any girl off her guard could easily be swept overboard by such a handsome man. He was obviously used to getting his own way where women were concerned and she would need to be vigilant!

'I'd let you ride Satan,' he was saying, 'but he's a mite frisky.'

'And you take it for granted that I couldn't handle him!' Now why had she said that? She hardly knew the front end of a horse from the back! Her only experience of riding had been four hack lessons when she was sixteen.

He stared at her serious expression and the pressure on her back increased. 'I beg your pardon, I didn't realise you were an accomplished horsewoman. Be my guest!' And he stood aside for her to mount.

Gemma burst out laughing to cover her embarrassment. 'I'm not an accomplished horsewoman. I can just about keep my balance on a quiet horse. It's the way you assumed I wasn't capable that's irritating.'

'Yes, I seem to irritate you a lot.'

After a few moments Shade asked, 'Did you enjoy the show the other night?'

'What I understood of it. You appeared to be enjoying yourself!' The moment she had uttered the words she could have bitten her tongue off. Oh, why did she have to give him the satisfaction of knowing she was interested in his activities with the brunette?

He treated her to an expression which could only be described as a smirk. 'Miranda? I told you, she's my cousin on a flying visit from Dallas. She left this morning.'

What a smooth-tongued liar he was! thought Gemma.

His hand moved up to the nape of her neck, sending a convulsive shiver snaking down her spine, and she jerked away from him. 'Can't you keep your hands to yourself?' she snapped.

'You're too jumpy for someone who professes to be

immune to physical contact,' he observed.

'Physical contact?' she asked scathingly. 'I call it mauling.'

They arrived at wide wooden gates standing open, with the words FIVE OAKS FARM emblazoned above them, and walked along a neat roadway between white-painted milestones until they reached a cluster of farm buildings.

Gemma glanced wryly at the four oak trees standing sentinel before the house.

'There used to be five, I assure you,' laughed Shade, 'but one was diseased and had to be removed. However, if you look closely you'll observe that we've planted a sapling in its place. In another hundred years or so the farm will be correctly named once more.'

The house was a low rambling building of grey and silver weathered granite with green ferns in the masonry. Its lattices and roof of small slates contributed to a nostalgic sense of the past. It had attractively carved gables and a verandah which ran the length of the frontage.

A stable boy appeared beside them and Shade handed over the reins of Satan with a few words as to the way the horse should be rubbed down. As he finished speaking a man came around the corner of one of the stables.

He addressed Shade in urgent tones. 'Cloud Pursued is in trouble, boss . . .' He noticed Gemma and hastily removed his stained Stetson. He was a giant of a man, even taller than Shade, in his late twenties, with broad shoulders and a muscled chest beneath his checkered shirt. His tough features were tanned and weatherbeaten and he had a shock of red hair and a shaggy moustache of a slightly darker colour.

'Have you called the vet?' Shade asked tersely.

'He's with her now. She might lose the foal . . .'

'Okay, keep me informed, will you?' Shade remembered his companion. 'This is Todd Ives, my right-hand man. Todd, Gemma Geary.'

Todd wiped his hand on his denim trousers and held it out to Gemma, while his expression remained grave. He studied her keenly for a moment, then forced his mouth into a smile that didn't quite reach his eyes. 'Pleased to meet you, miss.'

She fought down a desire to laugh. He was the nearest to a cowboy she had yet seen!

Shade took Gemma's elbow and steered her towards the stone steps of the farmhouse.

The sizeable hall had an attractive carved pine wainscot, while a long-case clock, which could only have been made in London, stood in the corner measuring the minutes with a comforting tick.

Shade called out to a passing maid to bring a tray of tea, then helped Gemma out of her jacket. As his hands glanced her throat she jerked away in alarm as if she had received an electric shock. She was disturbed to have been so strongly affected by his touch. Goodness, she didn't even like the man! She couldn't imagine what was the matter with her. It was as if some chemical reaction had been activated between them. That was it, she told herself, determined to fight the animal attraction which seemed to ooze from this dominant man.

He hung her jacket on a peg and allowed his gaze to travel slowly over her emerald sweater and tan slacks, his eyes lingering on the firm contours of her breasts and hips, before returning to her hot cheeks. She saw him run his tongue around his lips—like a cannibal savouring his next meal!

Chuckling to himself, he propelled her towards a doorway and ducked his head under the low lintel to usher her into a large sitting-room.

Leaving her side, he crossed the highly-polished floor, scattered with colourful rugs, to a woman seated, head bent, before an antique rosewood writing desk.

'Mother, this is Gemma Geary, Mrs Prescott's new companion.'

Mrs Lambert removed her reading glasses and leaned back in her chair. She was fiftyish, slim and elegant in a cream cashmere jumper and long brown skirt. Her hair, the same dark colour as her son's, but with touches of grey around the temples, was softly curled.

'So you're Gemma Geary!' The woman's eyes were particularly searching as she rose from her chair to offer her hand. 'Forgive me,' a smile darted about her mouth, 'but my son has spoken a great deal about you.'

Gemma shot a glance in Shade's direction.

'Do sit down,' invited Mrs Lambert as the tea arrived.

The two women seated themselves in armchairs beside the small occasional table while Shade stood sideways to the wide fireplace leaning his arm along the tall mantelpiece. The three of them engaged in small talk, but all the time Gemma was conscious that Mrs Lambert watched her intently. The lady wanted to know what Wimbledon was like, and the interior of Buckingham Palace, and Gemma had to admit that she had never seen either. The questions seemed innocent enough, but every now and then one of a more personal nature slipped in, like whether Gemma intended to make a career of her present job. Again she was able to answer quite truthfully that she had no idea.

Gemma's thoughts took wing as she wondered how many women Shade had ushered into this room to meet his mother. How many times had Mrs Lambert mused on whether this were *the* one? Did he bring them all home? Or did he bring none? Perhaps she, Gemma, was privileged. But then she was hardly a girl-friend . . .

Shade, placing his cup and saucer on the table, broke into her thoughts. 'I'll run you back to Clairmond now, if you're ready, Gemma.'

'Yes, please.' She shook Mrs Lambert's hand again. 'I have enjoyed meeting you. Thank you for being so hospitable to a weary traveller.'

In the hall they met Todd Ives, nervously twisting his hat in his hands. 'It's bad news, boss.'

'Okay, I'll come at once.' Shade turned to Gemma. 'I'm needed in the stables. Todd will drive you home.'

'But ...' began Todd, disappointment etching his voice.

'Do it!' said Shade.

The foreman shrugged philosophically. Before Gemma could offer any resistance, Shade placed his hand at the back of her head and brought his lips hard and swiftly to hers. Her mind was thrown into utter confusion and she had no time to remonstrate with him before he strode away out of the door.

She stared nonplussed at Todd Ives, who had lowered his gaze respectfully, but now met her eyes with a faintly amused expression.

'This way, miss,' he said, before leading her to the Range Rover at the rear of the house. The step of the vehicle was very high and she struggled in vain. He placed his hands on the seat of her slacks and, with a bashful 'Pardon me, miss', pushed her in.

He climbed into the driver's seat and threw an arm across her. Gemma shrank back in alarm, but he was merely reaching for her seat-belt. Help! She was over-reacting, she thought. Todd seemed intensely embarrassed and was all fingers and thumbs as he fastened the clasp about her. He had donned a grease-stained jacket and Gemma's nostrils were assaulted by the smell of horses and hay.

She looked across the yard and saw that her undignified antics had been witnessed by Shade. He waved and disappeared into a stable.

She glared after him. His kiss still stung her lips and she resented the fact that he had taken a further liberty with her. The kiss had been too swift for her to register any impression apart from indignation, and she was left with a sense of frustration.

Todd was uncommunicative on the journey and after several attempts to strike up a conversation—all to be met with a morose 'yep' or 'nope'—she gave up the effort. She could not help wondering what particular chip he carried on his shoulder.

She was relieved when they arrived on the forecourt of Clairmond, for she was tired and wanted a bath. Todd alighted from the wagon and walked round to open her door, then he half carried, half dragged her out.

'Would you like to come in for a coffee?' she felt obliged to ask.

He actually grinned, a rueful kind of expression that creased his hard-bitten cheeks. 'You don't know what you're asking, lady?

She stared at him, baffled.

He pondered for a moment, scratching his chin, then said, 'What the heck? Okay!'

Gemma raised her eyebrows, then walked up the steps ahead of him and entered the hall.

Mrs. Prescott was standing at the foot of the staircase, arranging some flowers in a bronze urn, and she turned to greet Gemma eagerly. 'You've been a long time ... ' She saw the young man and her expression froze. 'Todd Ives! What are you doing here? I thought I told you never to...'

Gemma said hastily, 'I asked him in for a coffee. He very kindly drove me...'

'Get out of this house!' Mrs. Prescott reached for her stick hanging on the banisters and shook it angrily.

The big man's lips tightened and he turned abruptly, wrenching open the front door and slamming it noisily after him.

Gemma stared askance at her employer. 'Whatever was all that about?' she asked.

'Todd Ives knows he's not welcome in this house!' said Mrs. Prescott, her lips compressed into a thin angry line. 'His father was a thief!'

'His father ...?' Gemma felt inclined to defend Todd all of a sudden. 'I don't see what that has to do with the son. Shade Lambert obviously thinks very highly of him.'

'Yes, and that's where we differ. Shade will be sorry! Blood will out!'

Gemma made her way to her apartment and, seeing the door of a small study standing open, ventured in to find Vikki replacing Mrs Prescott's newly-cleaned collection of Georgian silver.

Gemma looked round in admiration. There were at least a hundred items—the largest being a magnificent soup tureen engraved with cherubs and nymphs, the smallest a twisted mustard spoon.

'This collection must be priceless!' she exclaimed.

'Guess so!' Vikki smiled. 'Enjoy your walk?'

'Yes. I bumped into Shade Lambert and he took me to meet his mother.'

'You did?' exclaimed Vikki. 'Gee, count yourself privileged. How did she treat you?'

'She was friendly enough ...'

Vikki burst out laughing. 'Any new woman has to be weighed up as a potential daughter-in-law.'

'That's what I was thinking. But surely she knows by now that her son is a confirmed bachelor?'

'There's no such thing!' said Vikki sagely.

'Shade's foreman, Todd Ives, drove me home and I invited him in for coffee and ...'

'He was ordered off the premises,' finished Vikki. 'I should have warned you about that, but I didn't think you'd have cause to meet him.'

Gemma touched the petals of a silver rose entwined around a jug handle. 'What's the mystery?'

'The feud goes way back. The late Mr Prescott and the late Mr Ives were partners in a land reclamation scheme down in Mexico and both lost a great deal of money. I don't know much about it because it's a taboo subject in this house. Despite both protagonists being long since dead, the hatred flourishes still. Todd's father was made penniless as a result of the double-dealings, but Shade Lambert has befriended Todd.'

'So I really put my foot in it when I asked Todd in,' mused Gemma. 'He was about to refuse and then the devil got into him, I suppose.'

For the next week Gemma was involved with preparations for the banquet being held in Frankfort, the state capital, to honour Mrs Prescott, the president of a committee which had raised a million dollars for deprived children.

During the evening, various deserving youth leaders would be presented with medals. Her own committee was organising the event and, although Mrs. Prescott was to be the guest of honour, she insisted on doing her share of the preparations, which meant, in fact, that Gemma would be doing them.

Most of the organisation had been completed weeks ago and Gemma found it confusing coming in on the tail end of the thing, but she regarded this mission as a testing time. She was determined to do well and prove herself to be the perfect companion/secretary.

The preparations involved a great deal of time spent on the telephone and a trip into Frankfort, for which she managed to persuade Yarwood to let her drive the Cadillac. He insisted on accompanying her, however.

He was jealous of his responsibility for the lovely lilac car and watched her like a hawk. "Watch your speed!' he warned her. 'She's so smooth to drive that you don't realise the speed is building up and you might find it difficult to stop in an emergency.'

The banquet was being held in a large hall at the Civic Centre—only Gemma noticed it was spelt 'center'. She was reminded of the amount of Tippex Correcting Fluid she had used on Mrs Prescott's correspondence before she had got the hang of the vagaries of American spelling.

The ladies of the committee were energetic blue-rinsed matrons, delightful to work with and generous with their advice. Gemma had a feeling things were going to be all right.

'When it comes to putting on the style, you can't beat the Americans,' sighed Gemma as she and Vikki sat at the dining-room table patiently tying up two hundred little chiffon bags, all colours of the rainbow, containing fragrant dried herbs from Clairmond's famous herb gardens—these to be presented by Mrs Prescott to each lady guest as a memento of the banquet.

'Has Mrs Prescott found you an escort for the great night yet?' asked Vikki.

'Not as far as I know,' answered Gemma. 'Is it absolutely necessary for me to have an escort?'

'Oh yes, for a banquet of this size it's essential. Judge Dean will escort Mrs Prescott.'

The telephone rang shrilly and Gemma crossed to the sideboard to lift the receiver. 'Mrs Prescott's residence,' she said briskly.

'Gemma!' The tone was husky and sensual. 'How efficient you sound!' Unlikely as it seemed, Shade's telephone voice was even deeper than in real life.

As his honeyed tones washed over her entire body, she felt her scalp tingle and her toes curl up in her shoes.

'Speak to me, Gemma,' she heard him say coaxingly as the silent moments ticked by.

'I . . . I . . . What do you want, Shade?' She was aware that her voice shook and she turned her back on Vikki's probing gaze.

'Henrietta said you wanted an escort for the banquet and offered me first refusal.' His voice cracked on a note of laughter. 'I accepted, of course! Are you pleased?'

Another long pause. 'I . . . I . . .'

'You really must overcome that nasty stammer!'

She took a deep steadying breath. 'It's very kind of you, but can you spare the time to escort me?'

'Are you joking?'

'I'm surprised you have an evening free!' she said sarcastically.

'I'd break any date for you, Gemma! See you soon!' He laughed again and rang off.

Vikki opened her mouth to speak, but they were interruped.

'How are you two getting on?' Mrs Prescott came tapping her stick into the room. 'I'm sorry you're having to work so hard, Gemma, but all this is traditional. It must be hand-made and home-made.'

'And I thought it was the English who clung to tradition.' quipped Gemma.

Mrs Prescott took the chair at the head of the table and lit a cigarette. 'Well, I've solved the problem of your escort, Gemma . . .'

'I know!' She turned down the corners of her mouth. 'He's just telephoned with the news.' She felt her cheeks burning as she exclaimed, 'I do wish you'd asked me first!'

Mrs Prescott frowned. 'I thought you'd be thrilled. He's delighted to be of service. He assures me he's looking forward to the occasion immensely.

'And I have no say in the matter?' asked Gemma archly.

'He's the perfect escort, Gemma—so handsome. You'll be the envy of all the women.' Mrs Prescott noted her companion's flushed cheeks and laughed heartily. 'He's ideal for the job, my dear. A regular ladykiller and not likely to want to steal you away from me to lead you to the altar. I've got to be careful whom I place in your company. I don't want to lose you.'

'I keep telling you,' Gemma pointed out hotly, 'you won't lose me.'

'Ah, well it's always wise to be on the safe side,' rejoined her employer. 'Shade Lambert is no threat to my plans.'

For some inexplicable reason Mrs Prescott's words irked Gemma, and she wondered why this could be so. She was not the least interested in Shade Lambert. It suited her fine that he was not the marrying kind, because she would not marry him if he were the last man in the universe! He was too smooth, too arrogant, too aware of his sexual attraction to appeal to her. She preferred a gentler man, a man who was considerate instead of trying to score off a woman all the time—a man like Rowan. At once her heart gave that familiar painful lurch as she recalled their tender moments together. Oh, why was life so unfair . . .?

CHAPTER FOUR

THE auspicious day of the banquet arrived and Gemma took pains to look her best, trying on all her new gowns until she was satisfied with her reflection in the mirror. Her final choice was a dress of peacock-blue jersey, softly clinging to her firm curves, the full sleeves caught into a wide cuff at the wrists, the hem flouncing gracefully about her ankles. No bra was possible with this material and the neckline was scooped to give a glimpse of her cleavage.

She relented a little with regard to her hairstyle, still drawing the golden tresses back into a bun, but allowing the side strands to curl into wispy tendrils.

'You'll do,' she murmured, draping a filmy black stole about her shoulders and picking up a small black evening bag which matched her delicately-strapped high-heeled shoes.

She arrived at the top of the stairs to find her three companions for the evening standing in the hall below. For a moment a childish panic seized her. She heard Shade whistle admiringly as she began the descent.

'Sorry if I kept you waiting,' she gasped breathlessly.

'Well, you are making an entrance and no mistake!' observed Mrs Prescott sourly. 'May I remind you that I'm queen bee this evening!'

Gemma coloured slightly and almost missed her footing on the bottom stair. At once Shade was by her side, steadying her with one hand as his eyes travelled approvingly over the peacock-blue material.

Softly, so that Mrs Prescott could not hear, he said, 'You look beautiful.'

She saw that he looked splendidly virile and very sophisticated in a black tuxedo and bow tie.

'You look nice too,' she gulped weakly.

He produced a small corsage of gardenias from behind his back and proceeded to pin them to her dress, slipping his hand inside the top of the bodice.

His touch set her skin on fire and she felt her pulses quicken. 'Th ... thank you!' she exclaimed, flustered, pulling away from him.

'Well, you said you liked gardenias,' he explained.

'Did I? Oh ... yes!'

His eyes fell on the jade pendant at her throat. 'He's always with us, isn't he?'

Gemma smiled up at him and relaxed, on safe ground once more, as her sense of assurance surged back with a rush.

Mildred, the maid, was fussing over Mrs Prescott, who was dressed in a chartreuse satin evening gown, the gentle colour enhancing her regal bearing and complementing her upswept white hair. She wore a magnificent necklace of emeralds and her fingers were smothered with rings.

The Cadillac drew up at the front of the house and they all trooped down the steps. Yarwood wore his dress uniform, a dark brown outfit with gilt epaulettes and a sharply peaked cap. He saluted smartly as they got in and the staff, gathering on the steps, raised a little cheer as the party moved off.

'They're all mighty proud of you, Henrietta my dear,' said Judge Dean, seated beside Mrs Prescott on the back seat. 'And with good reason.'

Gemma sat beside Shade on the centre seat facing the others and she was conscious of his eyes on her, causing her to concentrate more than necessary on the passing scenery.

Yarwood drove sedately, taking thirty minutes to travel the twenty miles to Frankfort. While the judge regaled them with the details of a recent amusing court case, Gemma wondered just how deep was the friendship between him and her employer. He appeared a solid dependable character and was obviously fond of Mrs Prescott. They were so completely at ease in one another's company that a romance seemed possible, but perhaps Mrs Prescott, at least ten years the judge's senior, considered herself too old to embark upon marriage again, Gemma mused.

A cheering crowd awaited them at the Center, a host of elegantly dressed men and women all eager to shower their respect upon Mrs Prescott.

They were led inside the large hall to take their seats at the top table beside other distinguished members of the committee.

Gemma worked her way through artichokes à la grecque, game soup and sirloin béarnaise.

'Whatever am I doing here?' she asked Shade as he refilled her glass. 'I feel completely out of my depth.'

'You fit in very well,' he observed, a sensuous note creeping into his tone as his tawny eyes fell to her scooped neckline. 'Besides you're working, aren't you? This is your job.'

'But I've never helped organise anything on this scale before,' she wailed. 'I'm better at jumble sales.'

He raised his eyebrows, uncomprehendingly.

'I believe you call them thrift sales over here,' she rushed on. 'I do hope the presentations go off all right. I'm terrified in case I've overlooked something vital.'

'Well, it's too late now.' Shade laid his arm along the back of her chair. 'Forget it. Drink up and enjoy yourself.'

She felt his fingers lightly stroke her shoulder blade, sending a little shiver of excitement down the length of her spine.

She leaned forward to escape his touch, but there was no getting away from him. Trembling inwardly, she endured his caresses until the raspberry tart arrived and he was forced to employ his hands with fork and spoon.

'Do I bother you, Miss Geary?' she heard him whisper, and turned, scarlet-faced, to meet his wicked glance.

'You?' she enquired offhandedly. 'Not at all!'

'Ah, Gemma!' he sighed.

'Ah, Shade!' she mocked him. Then, 'Shade is an unusual name. Is it short for something?'

'No. My grandfather's name was Shadrach and it seemed kinda natural to christen me Shade.'

Gemma made a mental note to pass this information to her sister.

The long meal came to an end and a microphone was brought to the top table by a red-coated master of ceremonies.

Mrs Prescott rose to deliver her speech and Gemma handed her the typewritten pages, one at a time, as instructed. She felt she knew the speech as well as her employer, because they had rehearsed it thoroughly the past few days.

The recipients of the medals lined up and Gemma managed to see that each person received the correct award. Now came a surprise item not on the agenda— the presentation of a gold medal to Mrs Prescott herself. The applause was deafening and there was a standing ovation. Gemma was in on the secret and was the first to offer congratulations.

'You sure kept quiet about that,' said the old lady, moved to tears. 'Why didn't you warn me?'

'I was sworn to secrecy,' smiled Gemma, passing over a box of Kleenex.

It was her job also to see that Mrs Prescott was not overtired by too many wellwishers and photographers. When it became clear that she was flagging, Gemma, mindful of the old lady's habit of suddenly dropping off to sleep, suggested they leave.

'Good idea,' said Mrs Prescott. 'While we're ahead. Let's make a graceful exit and I can sleep in the car.'

And she did just that. Curled up on the back seat and covered with a rug, she dozed all the way home.

Judge Dean elected to sit beside the chauffeur to give his old friend more room, and this left Gemma and Shade alone to all intents and purposes, as there was a glass partition separating them from the front seat.

'You did your job beautifully,' said Shade, placing the tips of his fingers on Gemma's hand as it lay on the seat between them.

'Yes, you certainly know how to pick your secretary/companions,' she commented, acutely conscious of his nearness. She stared out into the darkness which was punctuated every few seconds by the main beams of passing cars.

She did indeed feel uplifted from the way the evening had gone off so smoothly, due in no small way to her own efforts. She experienced a feeling akin to intoxication which had nothing to do with the large quantity of wine she had consumed.

'I feel I've passed the test.' She gently withdrew her hand and fiddled with the straps of her bag. 'It's like winning the pools.'

Shade laughed quietly, once more baffled by her use of an English phrase.

'You're riding on the crest of success,' he commented. 'Why don't you let your hair down—and I do mean that literally.' He reached up and, before she was aware of his intentions, pulled out one of the jewelled grips.

She deftly stopped the tresses from falling about her shoulders, rummaged in her bag for a couple of spare grips and defiantly stuck them into her hair. 'I've told you before, it's none of your business how I wear my hair,' she said lightly.

'Scared?'

Her brows arched derisively. 'Don't make me laugh!'

Mrs Prescott gave a little moan in her sleep and Gemma bit her lip in consternation. 'You're wasting your time,' she whispered. 'I find your continual groping quite insufferable!'

'I find your continual groping quite insufferable!' he imitated softly, the American drawl detracting from the sharpness of her rebuke and making it appear comical.

Gemma could not help the little laugh which broke from her lips. Tonight she could forgive him anything.

They arrived at Clairmond and Mrs Prescott was hustled up the steps into the arms of the waiting Mildred. 'I'm going straight to bed now,' the old lady informed the others. 'I'll have one heck of a hangover in the morning. Gemma!' she called from the turn of the stairs. 'Give the gentlemen a nightcap before they leave.'

'I'll take a raincheck on that drink,' smiled Judge Dean with a yawn. 'I'm not as young as I was and these late nights don't do my ulcers any good.'

He bade them goodnight and Gemma cocked an enquiring eyebrow in Shade's direction.

'Yes, I'll take that drink,' he said enthusiastically, his eyes glinting with amusement at her undisguised reluctance to entertain him alone.

She preceded him to the drawing-room and busied herself at the cocktail cabinet. Presently she placed a brandy balloon in his hand. His fingers brushed hers on the glass and she jumped.

'To you!' he said, raising the bronze-coloured liquid.

He towered above her, dominating her senses, his sheer animal magnetism seeming to fill the room.

She crossed to the fireplace and, in her haste to put some distance between them, knocked against a jardinière of lilies, bruising the flowers and releasing their sickly perfume into the room. Steady, Gemma, she told herself, don't let him intimidate you!

Catching sight of herself in the mirror above the fireplace, she regarded her untidy hair and put up her hands to smooth it. 'Gosh, I look a mess! Thanks to you!'

Shade watched her reflection. 'Don't alter a thing on my account,' he drawled. 'You're beautiful with your hair all mussed up.' He gave her a long smouldering glance. 'The iceberg appears to have melted a little.'

She glared at him and sensed the colour flooding her cheeks. 'It's . . . late . . .'

He drained the glass and placed it carefully on the cabinet, then deliberately shortened the space between them until he stood close behind her. As she turned, the heady feeling washed over her again and she hiccupped. Covering her mouth with her hand, she gave him a little push, deriving an earthy pleasure from the smooth feel of his jacket. When he reached for her shoulders, she fell giggling into his arms. She felt the warmth of his body engulf her and was aware of a sensual male odour.

His kiss was swift upon her unsuspecting lips, but it was enough to send her senses swimming.

She gasped. 'Don't . . . please , . .' she murmured.

Once more Shade pulled her towards him, slowly teasing her bottom lip with his mouth, then claiming her with a possessive forcefulness.

Her feeble struggles were ineffectual as his hand slid behind her head, the pressure of his marauding mouth deliberately seeking her response and awakening in her body all sorts of unfamiliar feelings. She had never been kissed like this before. The knowledge poured over her like boiling honey, scalding her flesh and sending the blood pounding in her temples.

Holding her away momentarily, Shade forced his fingers into her untidy nest of hair and brought his lips to hers again. And again. When at last he let her go, Gemma was fighting for breath and dizzy from lack of oxygen.

His hands lightly touched her breasts, and she felt her nipples rise and push painfully against the material of her dress. 'There!' he whispered. 'Who said you were indifferent towards me?'

His words had an instant sobering effect on her. She took a step backwards, her confused thoughts milling around her brain in quick succession, as panic surged through her. What was she doing? With Shade Lambert of all people!

'It's late,' she said again, guilt overriding all other emotions. 'I must go to . . .' She broke off with embarrassment, reluctant to finish the sentence.

'Bed.' He supplied the last word. Surveying her from beneath half-closed lids, he murmured, 'Hm, the thought of your bed does something to me. Shall we round the evening off . . .?'

'I think not!' she snapped icily, recovering her poise and making a movement towards the door. 'You're not at all my type.'

'And what is your type?'

'I prefer a sensitive man.'

'Sensitive?' He sounded as if he had never heard of the word. 'Rowan was sensitive, was he?'

'Yes!'

'Did he take you to bed?' he asked bluntly.

'There are many ways of expressing love, Mr Lambert,' she said, refusing to be drawn, fully in command of her actions once more. 'You only appear to know one of them. I feel sorry for you.'

'You presume to know a lot about me.'

'Oh, shut up!' she snapped. 'You're hardly qualified to discuss a deep emotional involvement. You wouldn't understand in a thousand years.'

'And how many types have you known?' he persisted.

'I don't need to know any other types. Rowan was all I ever wanted.' She opened the door.

'Yes, tell yourself that, Gemma Geary. Run away upstairs and climb into your virginal bed, safe in the knowledge that you're still faithful to your dead sweetheart's memory.' Shade shook his head sadly. 'What a waste! You're capable of so much passion, as I've just discovered. That frigid exterior hides a spark just waiting to be kindled.'

'Well, it won't be kindled by you!'

'We'll see!'

Gemma noticed the bodice of her dress had become disarranged during their embrace, exposing more of her cleavage than she would have wished, but to straighten it now would only invite another jibe from him.

His eyes fastened on the tantalising gap in the garment, and suddenly he stretched out a hand towards her, but she twisted away from him, convinced she was about to be physically assaulted. But he had only reached for the pendant she wore, and the force of her evasive movements caused the chain to snap in two.

Tears sprang to her eyes. 'How dare you! You beast!' She snatched the pendant from his hand and felt around her neck for the broken chain.

He shrugged easily, giving the impression that he was well pleased with this turn of events. 'I hate the thought of that piece of metal standing between us.'

'Standing between us?' she echoed, unable to believe her ears. 'There's more than a jade necklace standing between us. Gosh, how conceited can you get! You fancy yourself, Shade Lambert!' With that she ran from the room as the tears splashed on to her cheeks.

When she reached her bedroom she was shaking with uncontrollable fury, not only with Shade, but with herself for allowing such an explosive situation to develop. She had already told herself that she had to be on her guard against such a man. Why hadn't she heeded the warning glint in his eyes?

'What does she mean, she can't stick Switzerland any longer and she's coming home?' demanded Mrs Prescott angrily.

'That was the telephone message,' Gemma said in exasperation. 'Elgiva said to tell you to expect her tomorrow afternoon.'

'Why didn't you call me to the phone?' asked Mrs Prescott. 'I would have told that young miss a thing or two!'

'She wouldn't hold on,' explained Gemma. 'She just delivered her announcement and hung up.'

'Oh dear,' said Mrs Prescott darkly. 'I'd hoped that very expensive school was going to perform miracles, but if she's quit in this underhanded fashion, then they've failed.'

Gemma imparted the news to Vikki as they sat together at the kitchen table. 'She sounds a right little monster. I'm dreading the thought of meeting her.'

Vikki sipped her coffee thoughtfully. 'Don't judge before you've met her. Mrs Prescott exaggerates her faults. Elgiva is a product of a failed marriage and a spoiled upbringing. You'll find yourself feeling sorry for her.'

'She sounds an enigma,' mused Gemma.

'I can understand her being fed up with Switzerland,' said Vikki. 'She's been there a year now. Mrs Prescott wouldn't even let her come home for Christmas.'

'What has she done that's so terrible?'

'Childish pranks,' said Vikki. 'At least that's how they're described around here. Mrs Prescott's granddaughter, you know! Anyone else would have been severely dealt with.'

'Such as?'

'You name it!' Vikki leaned her elbows on the table. 'She used to run with a wild bunch of kids. They threw crazy parties and got themsleves into a whole lot of scrapes. They were arrested once for shoplifting. They set fire to a horse barn . . .'

'Childish pranks indeed!'

'But that's just what they were,' insisted Vikki. 'And they all happened a long time ago. She's eighteen now and should be acting like a young adult. Besides, it isn't all bad news, honey. She can be quite charming when she wants to be.'

The house was thrown into an uproar by Elgiva's imminent arrival. From all the rumours, Gemma half expected the breakables to be carefully stowed away.

Gemma was at the top of the stairs when the girl entered the hall and had an opportunity to study the newcomer without being observed.

'Gee, it's good to be home!' exclaimed Elgiva, throwing her black pillbox hat on to a chair.

She was a vision of youthfulness and vitality, a tall willowy brunette with pert elfin features. As she slipped out of her leather coat she was revealed in an orange velour blouson worn loosely over yellow hip-hugging knee-breeches and extra-long tan suede boots, their high slender heels clicking over the marble tiles. Her outfit would have been totally outrageous on anyone else, but Elgiva displayed the flair and bearing of a young fashion model. Her skin was flawless, her make-up immaculate and her sleek hair unbelievably long.

As she turned to survey her grandmother, a smile flashed across her mobile features, first contrite, then teasing, then frankly sparkling with warmth. 'You're not going to be angry with me, are you, Gran?'

Mrs Prescott pursed her lips for long moments, then held out her arms.

A sigh of relief escaped Elgiva as she ran into them and kissed the old lady's cheeks.

Mrs Prescott's anger seemed to have burnt out. 'You're a naughty girl, Elgiva,' she said, trying to sound stern. 'I don't know what I'm going to do with you.'

Elgiva raised her elegantly-drawn brows disarmingly. 'But, Gran, I'm a reformed being! Can't you see how I've grown up?'

Yarwood staggered in with three suitcases and dumped them unceremoniously on the floor.

'This can't be all!' observed Mrs Prescott.

Yarwood glowered. 'There are twenty-seven more waiting at the airport!'

Elgiva threw back her head and laughed. As her eyes lifted to the stairs she caught sight of Gemma and asked, 'Who's this?'

Gemma hurried down the last of the stairs and was introduced.

'That's right, I remember, it was you who answered the phone,' said Elgiva, holding out a small well-manicured hand. 'Hi! I bet you've been bored ever since you arrived. But don't worry. From now on things will liven up!'

Elgiva's impact on the household was immediate, with the staff running around eager to do her bidding and Mrs Prescott waiting gloomily for 'something dreadful' to happen.

Under Mrs Prescott's guidance, Gemma organised a party in honour of Elgiva's return, to which all the local first families were invited. They arrived by the score, the men dressed 'old Southern' style, the ladies in the height of fashion, to eat, drink, talk and dance to music provided by a 'bluegrass band'. The courtyard was packed to capacity with expensive limousines and the house was ablaze with lights as the party took possession of the downstairs room and overflowed on to the terraces under the clement mid-April sky.

Elgiva looked sensational in a tight silver lamé dress, cut daringly low with the skirt split at the back from the top of her legs to her ankles. The men, young and old, were unable to keep their eyes off her as she glided provocatively across the room or abandoned herself wildly to one of the dances.

The dancing had been confined to the wide marble hall, and Gemma was fascinated by the foot-tapping quality of the raucous music. She had never been quite certain what 'bluegrass' meant and was surprised to find how simple it was. Just a string band—mandoline, banjo and fiddle—with no electronics whatsoever. The tunes reminded her of square dances back home in the village hall.

She knew Shade had accepted the invitation and was annoyed to find herself watching out for him to arrive, even though she dreaded the thought of confronting him for the first time since the banquet.

She was in her little office getting the small tape-recorder for Mrs Prescott, who had decided she wanted a record of the evening's entertainment, when she saw a car drive into the courtyard. She switched off the office light and, with her heart thumping rapidly, watched Shade climb out of a sleek black Porsche.

Gemma picked up the tape-recorder and hurried out of the room to seek safety among numbers back in the hall. She was halfway along the corridor when she almost collided with Shade as he entered unexpectedly through a side door.

She gasped as the colour mounted in her cheeks. He appeared unfamiliar in a white suit with matching waistcoat and a bootlace tie. He looked the perfect Southern gentleman, from the red kerchief hanging from his top pocket to his hand-sewn shoes. She thought, was this the same man who, with his kisses, had wreaked such havoc to her senses little more than a week ago?

He smiled intimately, his eyes raking over her blue silk Grecian-style dress and the string of aquamarines at her throat.

He took the tape-recorder from her hands and fell into step beside her. 'You look positively ravishing!' His eyes darted once more to the necklace and he lifted a puzzled eyebrow.

'The jade pendant that annoys you so much has gone in for repair,' Gemma reminded him stonily.

As they reached the hall, Mrs Prescott caught sight of

Shade and said petulantly, 'Where have you been? The party isn't complete without you.' She narrowed her eyes and exclaimed, 'Heavens, but you look handsome!'

'Sorry I'm late, my sweet,' he dropped a kiss on to her wrinkled cheek, 'but I've been having trouble with my mare, Cloud Pursued. I think we've saved the foal, but only time will tell.'

'Oh, I am pleased to hear that,' Gemma butted in, recalling how concerned Shade and Todd Ives had been about that particular mare.

'Gemma, see that Shade gets something to eat,' said Mrs Prescott.

Gemma preceded him to the deserted dining-room where long buffet tables had been laid with a varied selection of snacks. The dishes were sadly depleted now and the floor was littered with crumbs and paper napkins.

'What do you fancy?' she asked.

He laughed insolently. 'Anything you like!'

Gemma took up a plate and began to fill it, longing to escape his presence and return to the other room. A strange throb of excitement simmered just beneath the surface of her consciousness, making her all too aware of his proximity. It irritated her beyond all reason.

Suddenly she heard his sharp intake of breath and heard him exclaim, 'Wow! Who have we here?'

Gemma looked round and saw Elgiva standing in the french window, her waist-length hair disarrayed, her hands lightly resting on her silver lamé hips as she gazed from lowered lashes at Shade.

'Elgiva!' he breathed, stepping towards her. 'You've grown into a real beauty!'

She held her pose and flashed him a smile. 'Uncle Shade! Still as handsome as ever! And still unattached, I hear.'

'I waited for you to grow up, honey, like I promised,' he quipped. 'Gee, it was worth waiting for!'

She came towards him slowly and a wave of exotic perfume drifted into the room. With total lack of inhibition she slid her arms about his neck. 'It's good to see you, Uncle Shade.' She laughed. 'Say, I can't call you Uncle any more.'

Their lips met in a kiss and Gemma squirmed with embarrassment. She turned away and doggedly continued with her task of filling the plate with tidbits.

'Come and dance with me, lover!' drawled Elgiva, taking Shade's hand and dragging him to the door. 'I'm tired of dancing with all those uncouth youths. What I need is a real man.'

'But I was just about to eat,' protested Shade.

'Later!' said Elgiva. 'It's my party and you've got to please me.'

Shade shrugged apologetically at Gemma. 'Sorry! Don't bother with that plateful. I'm suddenly not hungry any more. Will you excuse us?'

With that he and Elgiva, arms entwined, left the dining-room.

Gemma angrily tossed the plate on to the table, not caring that the contents overspilled on to the cloth. Her pride had been dented. The fact that she detested Shade Lambert was neither here nor there. She felt she had been cast aside like the leftovers which surrounded her.

As she walked listlessly towards the hall, she thought that perhaps she would get some respite from Shade's attentions now that Elgiva had arrived on the scene. The realisation should have lifted her spirits, but strangely enough it had the opposite effect.

The band was playing a jerky waltz and the lights were dimmed. Shade and Elgiva were wrapped in each other's arms, barely moving, lost in their own little world.

'Come and make an old man happy, my dear.' Gemma allowed Judge Dean to lead her on to the floor, but all the time they were dancing, she could not keep her eyes from the gleam of the silver dress.

'What's the matter?' asked the Judge. 'Is that precocious miss giving you a hard time?'

'Of course not,' said Gemma lightly. 'I don't give a damn about Shade Lambert.'

Gemma was in great demand for the dancing and was taking a breather, an hour or so later, when Shade appeared at her side. He propelled her reluctantly towards the crowded dance floor as the band struck up a bright up-beat foxtrot.

She was unnerved by the way he placed his hand firmly against her back and moulded his figure closely to hers. He possessed a natural grace and hips that moved with the smoothness of a snake. He was a forceful, competent dancer, she discovered, and his movements completely dominated her as he spun her this way and that, never once causing her to falter. She felt like a rag doll being pushed about on wheels!

'What's the matter?' she enquired after a few moments. 'Has she given you up already?'

'Who?' he asked innocently.

'Elgiva, of course. My goodness, she certainly turned on the charm! You want to watch out or she'll be leading you up the aisle before you know it.'

'Not Elgiva! She was only joking, and so was I. Heck, she's still a kid!'

'You seemed very flattered by the way she greeted you,' persisted Gemma.

'Who wouldn't be? And you're jealous, are you?'

'Jealous? How ridiculous! You have a one-track mind.'

He chuckled into her ear and his fingers caressed her back through the thin material of the dress. In the muted light she noticed that his eyes took on the colour of tortoiseshell, and she cursed herself for her interest.

'How do you get on with Elgiva?' he asked. 'She must be quite an unsettling influence on the household.'

'You can say that again!' said Gemma with feeling. 'She's all right, really. I don't see much of her. She's enrolled with a secretarial college, which seems a little out of character.'

'A secretarial college?' he echoed. 'I wonder what she's up to now.'

The dance ended and Gemma felt someone touch her arm.

'So it was you who took my man away?' Elgiva's eyes flashed angrily at Gemma. 'Say, are we rivals for Shade? How cute!'

'No, we're not rivals!' said Gemma evenly, regarding the girl's lovely face and perfect skin. 'You're welcome to him!' And with that satisfying parting shot, she went in search of Mrs Prescott to see if there was anything she could do.

When she returned to the hall there was no sign of Shade. Elgiva was missing too.

Much later, Gemma went to the kitchen to ask Cook to prepare the coffee before the guests departed and found Vikki seated at the table sipping a beaker of milk. The housekeeper had been asked to work overtime to supervise the kitchen for the party.

'Thank goodness it's nearly over,' she yawned. 'These late nights interrupt my routine at home.'

Gemma went to the sink to pour herself a glass of water and glanced out of the narrow window overlooking the courtyard where the cars were parked. All at once she stiffened and let out a gasp.

'What have you seen?' asked Vikki, rising quickly. 'A prowler?' She gazed into the blackness of the night just in time to see the gleam of silver in the courtyard. 'Elgiva!'

They heard a man laugh, a deep throaty sound, then the silver glint disappeared between the vehicles.

'She's probably going to indulge in a necking session in one of the cars,' said Vikki.

'I shouldn't have thought a Porsche was all that roomy.'

'Porsche?' asked Vikki puzzled. 'Shade came in a Porsche, didn't he?'

'Yes, I believe he did,' said Gemma, trying to sound offhand.

A smile of understanding crossed Vikki's features. 'You have no proof she's with Shade.'

'I'm not bothered whether she's with him or not!' said Gemma heatedly. 'I wish you wouldn't all assume I'm interested in him.'

'All women are supposed to fall for his charms,' grinned Vikki. 'Why should you be any different?'

Shade and Elgiva had not returned by the time the party started to break up around midnight. As the guests drifted away in twos and threes, and the cars began roaring off down the drive, Gemma put on her stole and wandered out to get a breath of air that wasn't permeated with stale tobacco smoke and gin fumes. She purposely avoided going anywhere near the courtyard. She had no desire to stumble across Shade and Elgiva in the throes of passion.

She walked towards the other side of the house, picking her way along the little paths running between the renowned herb gardens, which were illuminated by the occasional lamppost.

It irked her to think she was not in control of her feelings. She had no intention of getting romantically involved again, least of all with Shade Lambert, so the sooner she stopped thinking about him the better. Shade Lambert, who had the reputation for breaking women's hearts! She needed him like a garden fête needs rain! 'They all fall for him'. Well, she would be the exception that proved the rule.

She had reached another little courtyard, where Yarwood sometimes carried out car repairs, and was surprised to see, in the gloom, the outline of an old

Packard car. She almost bumped into it before she saw
the gleam of the chromium fittings. She idly wondered
what it could be doing here. Perhaps it was something
Yarwood was working on in his spare time, but it looked
far too dilapidated for him to bother with, he was so
proud of the Cadillac.

While she stared, someone in the front seat put a light
to a cigarette. As the match flared, she recognised the
shaggy red moustache of Todd Ives. A moment later
the engine throbbed to life and the headlights came on,
before the car moved off along the path towards the
drive.

Whatever was he doing? A worried frown creased
Gemma's forehead. He had been ordered off the
premises by Mrs Prescott, yet he had been here in the
courtyard. Was he waiting to drive Shade back to Five
Oaks? No, Shade had come in the Porsche.

Gemma pondered the puzzle as she prepared for bed.
At least it stopped her thinking about Shade Lambert.

'I'm in love!'

Elgiva paused for effect in the doorway of the dining-
room the following morning to proclaim the news.

'Already?' asked Mrs Prescott, eyeing Elgiva with a
jaded expression. The lady had over-indulged with the
wine the night before and was having a little stewed
fruit for breakfast instead of her usual waffles. 'You've
only been home four days.'

'Time has nothing to do with it.' Elgiva smoothed the
seat of her blue jeans and slid into the chair. Today she
looked positively childlike, thought Gemma, with fresh-
scrubbed face and hair drawn back into a ponytail, her
fluffy angora sweater emphasising her firm young
breasts.

'Who's the lucky guy?' asked Mrs Prescott.

'Shade, of course,' said Elgiva.

'Bit sudden, isn't it?' asked her grandmother. 'On the

strength of one evening? You were only a kid when you went away.'

'What has that to do with it?' asked Elgiva, spooning a generous helping of honey on to her plate. 'It was love at first sight. We just looked into each other's eyes and wham, that was it!'

'Now, he would be a catch!' observed Mrs Prescott enthusiastically. 'I would approve of that. But I doubt if any girl could tie him down. You'd just become another in his long line of conquests.'

'Hold on! Who said anything about tying him down?' A dreamy look came into Elgiva's eyes. 'Still, it's not a bad idea at that. I shall work on it. He's taking me to the disco in Lexington tomorrow night, and then there's the steeplechase on Saturday . . .'

'You might just pull it off,' said Mrs Prescott. 'I saw the impact you made on him last night. One look at you and he went down like a poleaxed bull! If anyone can do it, then you can.'

'I always saw him as Uncle Shade,' giggled Elgiva, 'but not any more.' She caught Gemma's eye and winked. 'Looks like it's every woman for herself.'

'What do you mean?' asked Mrs Prescott, intercepting the wink.

'I think our English friend is sweet on him too!' drawled Elgiva.

Gemma, blushing furiously, concentrated on sugaring her coffee.

'Oh, stop embarrassing the girl,' said Mrs Prescott. 'Gemma is far too level-headed to fall for a man like Shade!'

CHAPTER FIVE

'IT must be quite a gruelling race if it takes an hour,' remarked Gemma, helping Mrs Prescott to a seat in the front row of chairs in the Dutch barn.

'It sure is,' said the old lady, handing her stick to Gemma. 'The men race across country on a complicated course around the tobacco plantations, doubling back and looping some areas again. We call it the Golden Gloryboys Trail after my husband's most illustrious brand of tobacco. Wayne thought up the idea for an annual horse race, forty years ago, and I've carried on the custom ever since he died. The prize of one thousand dollars always goes to charity, but the winner keeps the cup for a year. I'm glad it's raining. It makes it more interesting when the course is waterlogged,' she added wickedly.

Gemma hung her umbrella on the back of her chair and stared about her with interest. The open-sided barn, situated in a small field the other side of Lexington, was packed to capacity and the inclement weather had not deterred a great crowd of spectators from milling about on the wet grass.

The magnificent silver cup, crowned with a smoker's pipe, stood on a small table in front of the barn, along with a magnum of champagne.

Gemma wore her yellow raincoat and waterproof boots and had loosely draped a long chiffon scarf printed with a blue floral design around her neck in accordance with instructions from Vikki. 'You must wear a scarf. It's traditional,' the housekeeper had said the day before. 'Each rider wears a lady's favours for the race. It's a great honour if someone asks to wear yours.'

Thirty or so contestants had assembled in front of the barn, some already mounted, others leading their horses by the reins. Gemma saw Shade and Todd Ives talking together as the latter made an adjustment to his roan's girth-strap. Both men wore black slickers.

'Just look at that Ives fellow!' muttered Mrs Prescott belligerently. 'The nerve of him, to enter this race!'

'Be fair,' said Gemma, springing to Todd's defence. 'You told me the race was open to anyone living in the district.'

'I'd rather die than hand him the prize,' glowered Mrs Prescott. 'Why, my husband would turn in his grave!'

'Better pray he doesn't win, then,' said Elgiva.

'Oh, he won't win.' Mrs Prescott sounded quite confident. 'We all know who'll win. The same person who always wins!' She looked up and smiled at the approach of Shade, leading his horse, Satan, by the reins. 'We were just talking about you. Have you come to claim my scarf?'

'Oh no, you must take mine!' cried Elgiva, undoing her scarlet square and holding it out to him.

'Elgiva, show some respect for your elders,' said Mrs Prescott crossly. 'Shade, I insist you wear mine!'

Shade looked from one to the other of them, then with a helpless shrug turned to Gemma. 'The only way I can get out of this delicate situation is to take yours,' and he whipped her scarf away. Stupefied, she watched him knot it about his throat as an inexplicable tingle of excitement suffused her body.

He swung easily into the saddle and raised his hand to her before cantering away.

'Oh, Gran, you are a nuisance,' cried Elgiva. 'I wanted Shade to wear my favour, and you've spoilt everything! I'll get even with you!' She tossed her head angrily and looked about her as if seeking some mischief with which to pay her grandmother back. Her eyes lighted on Todd Ives, standing a little way away from them. 'I'll give my scarf to your *bête noire*,' she announced, standing up and moving towards him.

'Don't you dare!' Mrs Prescott shouted out the order. Her voice sounded so ominous that Gemma jumped and Elgiva stopped in her tracks.

For a moment the girl paused, appearing to consider the pros and cons of defying her grandmother, then, obviously deciding it was not worth it, sulkily returned to her seat.

Todd had witnessed the little scene and for one instant there was such a fierce glint in his eyes that Gemma caught her breath. But it was only a fleeting reaction and, in a moment, his face was impassive again.

'There! Look at him!' scowled Mrs Prescott. 'Did you see that look he gave me? I reckon just then he could have murdered me!' She swung round on Elgiva. 'Stop misbehaving yourself! We don't want any incidents.'

Two clean-cut young men whom Gemma recognised as guests at the recent party rode up to claim Elgiva's and Mrs Prescott's scarves, just as Judge Bradley Dean warned, over the megaphone, that the riders had better hurry and line up. Almost immediately there came the crack of a starting pistol. The horses reared, then raced away through the wide gateway to disappear from sight.

The centre of the meadow was given over to a brass band display, and vendors moved among the crowds with snacks.

'If you'd given your scarf to that odious man, I'd have disinherited you, Elgiva, I swear!' declared Mrs Prescott when they had been served with plastic cartons of coffee. 'Supposing he'd won? You would have had to ride with him in the buggy for the lap of honour, and a fine spectacle that would have made—Prescott and an Ives riding together!'

Gemma digested this information. That meant if Shade won then she would be expected to do the lap of honour with him. And he was expected to win! Another tingling sensation ran down her spine.

'Isn't it boring now the men have ridden away?' said Elgiva, biting into a hot dog. 'My man, Shade, anyway.'

'Your man?' asked Mrs Prescott with sudden interest. 'So you already see Shade as your man?'

Elgiva smiled enigmatically. 'But you've spoilt everything, Gran. I won't be the one to ride in the buggy with him. That honour will go to Gemma.'

'Well, I'm sorry if I spoiled your plans,' said Mrs Prescott, 'but I'm sure you won't let a little thing like that deter you from making him your abject slave.'

Gemma closed her ears to the conversation and made an effort to concentrate on the drum-majorettes now cavorting about the damp meadow.

By the time they had finished their display the rain had eased off and the grass began to steam in the heat of the sun. Presently there came the frantic buzz of voices:

'The first rider's in sight!'

'It's Shade Lambert!'

'He's knocked seven minutes off his previous record!'

A cheer went up as the mud-spattered horse and rider raced into the field to come to a halt before the barn. As he dismounted he was besieged by photographers and reporters from the local papers.

Within minutes the rest of the riders had returned to the meadow and each was greeted enthusiastically. Gemma noticed that Todd Ives was fourth.

Mrs Prescott presented Shade with the cup and the champagne, then delivered a few words of congratulations. Shade replied that the cheque would go to the Distressed Jockeys Fund, which information brought a roar of noisy approval from the crowd.

Shade expertly removed the cork from the bottle and poured the golden effervescing liquid into the cup. He drank deeply, then, egged on by the crowd, poured the rest of the wine over his head. It all seemed to be a well-versed ritual, observed Gemma.

The band struck up 'Camptown Races,' and a flower-decked buggy, pulled by a bright-eyed pony, was led on. Shade peeled off his waterproof slicker and handed it to Todd, then took giant strides towards the barn and held out his hand to Gemma.

She rose shyly, cursing the blush that so easily rose to her cheeks. He seized her hand in an iron-hard grip and jerked her into his arms, almost knocking her off her feet so that she was forced to cling to him to keep her balance.

He towered above her, larger than life, smothering her senses with his masculinity, and the crowd went wild as he kissed her heartily. She knew he was flushed with victory and that any girl whose scarf he wore would have received the same treatment, nevertheless, the feel of his hard mouth on hers sent her heart fluttering. Lord, she thought, she was reacting like a teenager!

Shade laughed triumphantly, then picked her up in his arms and began to walk towards the buggy.

'Put me down, you idiot!' she hissed, as a fount of hysteria welled up inside and threatened to swamp her.

'Be quiet!' He dumped her unceremoniously into the buggy. 'It's traditional!'

He took the reins and they set off around the field at a spanking pace to the tumultuous cheers of the spectators.

When Gemma had caught her breath she stole a glance at the man beside her. There was a wild gleam in his eyes, his cheeks glowed and his jaw jutted aggressively. He smelt strongly of horses, sweat and Dom Perignon.

'This tradition business!' she said scathingly, holding on tightly to the side of the buggy as they approached a corner.

'Actually it's not tradition to carry the girl, but you

were not to know,' he admitted with a grin.

'Oh, you trickster!' she scolded. 'Whatever will Elgiva think?'

'Elgiva? What has she to do with it?'

'She's keen on you.'

'Is she? Well, it will do her good to think she has some competition,' he replied with relish.

'But she has none!' Gemma bit her lip pensively. Was that why he had done it? To make Elgiva jealous?

'No?' he asked as they arrived once more at the barn. A stable boy ran forward to take the pony's head and Shade helped Gemma out of the buggy.

Judge Dean announced that the meeting was over and the crowd began to drift away. Soon a steady stream of horse boxes filled the exit from the meadow.

Shade still had tight control of Gemma's hand and now he pulled her out of the way of the jostling crowd surging past them, into the comparative privacy of a space between two coaches which had been used to transport the band.

He undid the long chiffon scarf he still wore and slipped it around her neck, drawing her resolutely towards him. 'Okay, now we'll do it right,' he whispered. Before she could protest he cupped her face in his hands and brought his mouth deliberately to hers. As he expertly parted her lips with the tip of his tongue she received an intense shock like forked lightning ripping through her, and was overtaken by a mixture of contradictory yearnings—wanting to get away from him, wanting to stay!

Shade held her at arms' length and from the way he panted he could have just scaled Annapurna! Gemma watched his heaving chest and noticed that little black hairs had worked their way through the buttonholes of his tight cheesecloth shirt. The sight of them sent a rash of goosepimples erupting over her skin. Somehow she dragged her eyes away.

A man with a big bass drum came by and the two of them were pushed together again. 'Come and have dinner with me,' Shade urged.

'I'm . . . I'm . . . I've got to go . . . go home with Mrs Prescott,' Gemma stammered. He was too close for her to think clearly!

More bandsmen invaded their privacy and Shade led Gemma towards his Range Rover where Todd Ives was getting the two Five Oaks horses into the towed box, watched by Elgiva.

Gemma drew enough strength from the girl's presence to tell Shade firmly, 'Thank you for the invitation, but the answer is no.'

'Where have you two been?' Elgiva darted a look of animosity at Gemma. 'I hope you enjoyed the buggy ride, Gemma. But you must have—Shade's such a gorgeous hunk of man.' She slipped her arm through his, drawling, 'Honey, are you taking me to dinner?' She stood on tiptoe and whispered something in his ear.

'Sure, kid. Anything you say,' he grinned.

'Stop calling me kid,' she pouted crossly. 'I'm not a kid, I'm a woman. You should know that, of all people.'

'Sure do!' he replied. He glanced across at his foreman. 'All set, Todd?'

'All set, boss.'

Shade bade Gemma good day and Elgiva was hauled, giggling, into the back seat of the Range Rover. Moments later Gemma watched them drive off, Elgiva cradling the silver cup in her lap and laughing up at Shade, who sat beside her, while Todd Ives sat in the front seat gloomily gripping the steering wheel.

There, Gemma congratulated herself, it had not been too difficult to resist Shade's invitation. She had done the right thing. Then why did she feel so miserable?

'Eating your heart out?' It was Judge Dean surveying her kindly.

Gemma affected a yawn. 'I wish you'd all play another record.'

The Judge watched her with an air of quiet amusement, 'I've seen the way you look at him, my dear. You go all to pieces whenever he's near you. You blush and stammer . . .'

'Because he unnerves me!' cried Gemma, shaken by this reasoning. 'He won't take no for an answer. It's as if I'm under constant siege!'

Gemma travelled back to Clairmond in the Cadillac with Mrs Prescott and the Judge and spent the evening watching television with them. By nine o'clock Elgiva had not returned. Gemma decided on an early night and made her way to her apartment. She intended writing some letters home, but could not concentrate. She kept recalling the feel of Shade's arms about her and the Judge's disturbing words.

Other thoughts came unbidden into her mind. Elgiva had said 'You know I'm a woman, Shade'. She could be showing off. On the other hand, they could be lovers.

Gemma rose from her chair and walked listlessly into the bedroom. What was it about Shade that made her so sensitive to everything concerning him? Why did every glance, every gesture make such an impact on her mind? It was as if he had mesmerised her so that whenever they met she was fighting against a powerful attraction. But how was that possible? She liked nothing about him, he was far too arrogant, far too sure of himself.

Then suddenly she knew the answer. It was because of what he was capable of, the fact that he could destroy her detachment and force her to—love him!

She lay down on the bed to work out her plan of campaign. The thought of doing battle with him was exhilarating. She would not fall under his spell. She would be strong in resisting him . . .

She fell asleep lying on the bed still fully dressed and

was awakened some hours later by the light from the full moon shining directly upon her face. She struggled up and glanced at the little ebony and gilt clock on her bedside table. It was three o'clock.

She swung her feet on to the floor and went to the small curtained recess in the sitting-room to make herself a cup of tea. Returning to the bedroom, she placed the cup on the dressing table and went to the window to draw the curtains. Outside, the moonlight had turned night to day and the garden beneath her looked eerily bright.

Then all at once a movement caught her eye. Someone was walking across the lawn from the terraces—a tall man carrying a Stetson hat. Gemma had no doubt whatsoever that it was Todd Ives. As she watched he threw the hat into the air and caught it again.

What does he want, prowling around? she thought. What was the matter with the man? Could it have anything to do with his father's feud with Wayne Prescott? Gemma shivered involuntarily, wondering if she should acquaint Mrs Prescott with what she had seen. She had kept quiet about seeing him in the little courtyard the other night, but his trespassing was getting to be a habit.

On the other hand, she did feel sorry for Todd and did not wish to get him into any unnecessary trouble. After all, he wasn't to blame for his father's shortcomings. Perhaps it would be best to mention it to Shade and get his reaction first.

She decided she would talk to him about it the next time they met—whenever that might be. She experienced a thrill of pleasurable anticipation at the prospect, and smiled wryly to herself as she realised her newly-formed plan of campaign was already in jeopardy.

Gemma tore the page off the little loose-leaf calendar on the writing desk in her sitting-room and caught her breath as a deep sense of misery engulfed her. It was the twenty-first of April. How could she have let Rowan's birthday creep up on her so stealthily? It was also the day they had become engaged—was it only three years ago? It seemed much longer, another dimension, so much had happened to her since then. She tried to picture his beloved face, but the memory eluded her.

Shocked to the core and riddled with guilt, she hurried into the other room to pick up the photograph she kept beside her bed. Rowan's image smiled tenderly back at her and she traced her fingers over his sensitive mouth, the thoughtful hazel eyes and that uncontrollable mop of soft brown hair.

She replaced the frame on the bedside cabinet and clasped her burning cheeks. She always approached this day with reverence, she thought; how could she have forgotten?

She needed something of Rowan's to touch, and felt for the pendant before she remembered that it was still being repaired. The jewellers had had to send to Mappin and Webb in London for a special clasp replacement, and it might take weeks.

Feverishly she rummaged in the drawer of the dressing table, taking out the beribboned bundles of well-worn letters and cards until she found the slim book of Keats' poems which Rowan had given her just before he died. She felt the tears crowding her eyes and tried to blink them away, but the dam burst and she gave herself up to weeping.

A long time later she slipped the book into the pocket of her skirt and pushed the other items back into the drawer, resisting the temptation to delve into their intimate contents and wallow in her grief. With a heavy heart she descended the stairs.

For days now she had been busy with preparations for the forthcoming children's pageant due to be held on May Day, but today she found it difficult to get her

brain to work and decided instead to clean out one of
the cupboards in the office. It had been used to store
items and literature which Mrs Prescott had collected
from her charitable work over the years.

Gemma tied a scarf over her hair and got down on
her knees to remove all the accumulated books, pamph-
lets and photographs, then, sitting among the untidy
piles, she sorted everything out into relevant bundles
and tied them together with string. It was a dusty business
and her throat was crying out for liquid when Mildred
arrived with a mug of coffee.

They exchanged a few words of greeting, then the
maid left and Gemma dropped into her chair. She sipped
the coffee gratefully, then reached into her pocket for
the book of poems, turning automatically to the one
entitled 'Isabella', where Rowan had used red ink to
underline certain passages:

'Parting they seemed to tread upon the air,
     Twin roses by the zephyr blown apart,
     Only to meet again more close.'

Fresh tears welled up in her eyes and overflowed down
her cheeks. She let them fall unchecked, watching with
morbid fascination as they spotted the page of the book.
She jumped at the slight sound beyond the door and
was annoyed when it opened to reveal Shade.

'My dear!' His expression was sympathetic. He
crossed to her side and placed one hand lightly upon
her shoulder. 'What's the matter?'

'Oh, go away!' blubbed Gemma, wriggling free from
his grasp. She felt so foolish. This was all she wanted,
for him to see her cry. 'Don't you ever knock?'

He looked puzzled and reached for the book, silently
taking it from her hands and flicking over the pages to
read the inscription on the fly-leaf—'For ever, Rowan'.

'I might have known.' He bent over and caught
one of her tears on his finger. 'Sitting here getting yourself into a state . . .'

She wiped at her eyes and cheeks with her hands and endeavoured to collect herself. 'It's Rowan's birthday,' she explained, 'and the day we got engaged. I'm afraid the memories were just too much for me to handle.' She added acidly, 'However, I wouldn't expect you to understand.'

'You're living in the past,' he said, his voice kind. 'Do you honestly intend to stay faithful to a ghost till the end of your days?'

'It isn't a question of staying faithful,' she said, snatching the book away and throwing it into a drawer. 'It's a question of being spoiled for anyone else.'

'Perhaps you should give someone else a chance and see,' he said softly, bending over her again.

'I don't want to!' Her voice was becoming hysterical. 'I'm sick to death of people trying to . . .'

'But relationships can't flourish unless they move forward,' he reasoned tenderly. 'Love for a dead man is sterile.'

Gemma considered this for a moment.

'What was so special about him?' asked Shade, sounding genuinely interested. 'What made your relationship so unique?'

'Well, we never quarrelled, for a start . . .'

'Never? How dull! Never to have seen your lovely blue eyes flash in anger . . .!'

She jumped up from her chair to move the filing box noisily about on the desk. 'I'm not listening. Go away!'

He seized her chin and twisted her head round so that she was forced to meet his amber gaze. 'Rowan missed a lot! I enjoy our volatile exchanges.'

'It's different with us!' She stared back defiantly. 'I'm not in love with you!'

Shade let her go.

She gave a derisive laugh. 'If you only knew how wrong you are about Rowan and me!' Her shoulders slumped suddenly. 'Oh, what's the use trying to explain to you?'

He stared at her tear-wet lashes and dust-streaked cheeks, and an expression of infinite pity crossed his features to acknowledge the torment she was suffering. 'Look, why don't you come out riding with me? It would do you good to get into the fresh, clean air. I have a nice gentle mare . . .'

'No, I can't. I'm busy.'

'Of course you can,' he said persuasively. 'Mrs Prescott won't mind if you take the rest of the day off. I'll tell her you're not feeling well.'

'No! I don't want to. Go and ask Elgiva. She hasn't gone to college today.'

'Why ever should I want to take Elgiva riding?' he asked, puzzled. 'I don't know where you picked up this idea, but I assure you there's nothing between Elgiva and me.' A sly grin spread over his face. 'Why are you so scared to come riding with me? Can't you trust your-self to come for a little ride—in daylight—where there are bound to be other people around? Don't you think you can resist me?'

'Oh, you never give up, do you?' She stared at him wide-eyed. 'You'd like to think I can't resist you!'

'Prove it, then!' He paused. 'I warn you, I shan't go away until you agree to come.'

'Right, I will! I'll show you, Shade Lambert! Then perhaps you'll leave me alone.'

He gave a little bow. 'I accept the challenge.'

'But I've nothing to wear,' she cried, immediately re-gretting her impulsive acceptance of his invitation and trying to think of a reasonable excuse not to go. 'I have no riding gear . . .'

His eyes swept over her blue silk blouse and Black Watch tartan skirt. 'Don't you own a pair of jeans? Or perhaps Vikki could find you a pair. We're only going for a gallop, it's not the Kentucky Derby.'

Gemma knew she was beaten. 'All right.'

He patted her shoulder. 'Run along and wash your face.'

'My face?' She stared in horror at her reflection in the tiny mirror on the shelf and saw the dusty smudges. 'Oh, why didn't you tell me I looked such a mess?'

'You always look good to me,' he grinned. 'Run along and change and I'll square it with Henrietta. Meet you outside in fifteen minutes.'

He strode away in search of Mrs Prescott and Gemma sped up the stairs. With trembling fingers she pulled off her skirt and went to the wardrobe for her jeans and short black velvet jacket. Throwing them on the bed in readiness, she went into the bathroom to wash her face and apply a touch of make-up.

Standing by the window, brushing her hair into a thick coil at the back of her head, she glanced out to see Shade and Mrs Prescott, in earnest conversation, emerge from the side door and stroll into the sunshine. As they reached the lush green terraces, Shade placed his heel on the low parapet and said something that made Mrs Prescott giggle.

Everything about him was sensual, thought Gemma, every move whether calculated or not, emphasised his animal magnetism. The man simply could not help oozing charm. Right now it was oozing all over Mrs Prescott, who was old enough to be his grandmother! As he threw back his head and guffawed, Gemma hastily withdrew from his line of vision.

A sudden tightness seized her throat. Not since Rowan had her mind spun so habitually around a man, or her body responded so positively to the touch of a hand. She wished she hadn't risen to the bait and agreed to go out with him, but it was too late now. He had accepted the challenge! All she had to do was keep her head and guard against his obvious physical attraction.

That should be easy—on Rowan's birthday. She glanced again at the photograph and the breath shuddered painfully in her throat as pangs of loneliness and memories of all she had lost swept over her.

She found Shade waiting for her in the courtyard, leaning nonchalantly against the door of the Range Rover.

'You're late,' he greeted her. 'Having second thoughts?'

She tossed her head. 'Not at all.' She eyed the vehicle distastefully. 'Why did you have to bring that horrid thing? It's so difficult to get into.'

He manhandled her into the front seat and said slyly, 'I always use this wagon when I'm transporting women. It makes things kinda interesting!'

'Oh, you!' She thought for a moment. 'So it wasn't a spur-of-the-moment thing, your inviting me out?'

'Oh dear, I've been found out.'

The enclosed atmosphere of the vehicle brought out the flowery aroma of her perfume and she saw him sniff appreciatively. She wished then she hadn't put it on. It had been from force of habit, she told herself, but Shade was so vain he was bound to think she was deliberately seeking to encourage him by every subtle means at her disposal.

Within a few minutes they had arrived at Five Oaks, where Gemma was subjected to the further indignity connected with alighting from the vehicle.

All was hustle and bustle in the stable yard—men leading horses, others carrying buckets of water and bales of straw. Gemma breathed in the strong smell of hay and was reminded of home. She could hear the horses moving about in their stables and some of them poked their heads over the wooden half-doors, inviting her to stroke their soft noses.

There were 'No Smoking' signs everywhere. 'A fire here would be calamitous,' said Shade.

The men nodded amiably to Shade and eyed Gemma

curiously, returning her smile with warmth and friend-
liness.

Two boys were mucking out one of the stables and
clouds of dust billowed out into the yard. Gemma
coughed as it penetrated her lungs.

A tall man stepped from the grain barn and she
recognised Todd Ives. He wore leather gloves and a
quilted jerkin, and chaff was clinging to his cord
trousers. He stared at her for a moment, then removed
his hat, allowing the sunlight to glint on his red thatch
of hair. To her great surprise, he grinned at her.

'Hi, miss!'

'Hi!' she returned. She was at once reminded of his trespassing antics on the day of the race and was determined
to mention it to Shade as soon as they were alone.

Some physically handicapped children were taking a
riding lesson in one of the paddocks and Gemma leaned
on the fence to watch them.

'It's good for their morale,' explained Shade. 'Once
they get astride a horse they're as mobile as normal
children.'

A little group of tourists came around the side of the
stables, and Gemma recalled how Vikki had told her
that some of the horse farms were open to the public at
certain times. They were accompanied by an elderly
member of Shade's staff, a tall, sparse man with piercing
blue eyes.

'Bert refused to retire, so we've given him this job,'
Shade whispered to Gemma.

The man was reeling off a list of facts and figures and
Gemma learned that all the colts and fillies were the
result of carefully planned matings.

One of the tourists, a middle-aged woman, was
endeavouring to take a photograph of Bert and she
accidentally backed into Shade, dropping her camera
into a pile of hay. It was her fault entirely, but she
rounded angrily on Shade, unaware who he was.

Gemma watched in admiration as he calmly retrieved the camera, whispered something to the woman and smiled, completely disarming her so that her angry words melted on her lips. It was another example of his overpowering charm! Women just didn't stand a chance, thought Gemma.

'Whatever field of performance these horses enter, they prove that the term 'Kentucky-bred' means real quality,' Bert was saying proudly, aware that his boss was listening. 'A stallion generally serves thirty-two mares.'

The men in the group chortled and the ladies tittered with embarrassment. Gemma saw Shade watching her, one thick eyebrow raised quizzically, and she blushed.

He led the way to another stable yard and Gemma read a little framed notice affixed to the first stall. It was entitled 'The Horse Breeder's Prayer' and went on:

'St. George, thou saintly chevalier,
    With all my heart I implore thee,
    To mares and stallions thou art dear—
    Secure a favor for me.
    See here! My blood congeals with fright;
    The pedigree grand mare is foaling.
    Give her the best of foals tonight
    And send my cares a-rolling.'

'Are foals usually born at night?' enquired Gemma.

'More often than not,' grimaced Shade. 'And spring is our busiest time. Mares decide when they'll produce their foals and we're at their beck and call twenty-four hours a day. In the final weeks they have to be watched constantly in case problems arise. The times I've had to get out of my warm bed!'

Gemma was prompted to ask, 'How is Cloud Pursued? You told Mrs Prescott you thought you'd save the foal.'

He pointed to a little paddock where a white-maned chestnut horse nibbled the grass. 'There she is. Still hanging on to the foal, I'm thankful to say.'

A stable boy appeared with a grey horse for Gemma and held its head while she mounted into the saddle.

'Fantasy is the most placid horse I own,' said Shade, adjusting Gemma's stirrups. 'Just sit tight and let her set the pace. She'll keep abreast of Satan and me.'

Nervously Gemma looked down from her high position. She had only ridden hacks from the local riding school and had forgotten everything she had ever learned.

Shade swung on to the powerful black stallion and proceeded at a steady trot out of the stable yard towards the fields. As Fantasy followed suit, Gemma began to relax.

Shade quickened the pace by urging Satin to a gallop and they crossed three fields, passing jeeps and riders and men repairing fences. Horses grazed everywhere. They splashed through a river and came to a peaceful valley where a big stretch of water reflected the majestic hills beyond.

'This is limestone soil,' said Shade, after they had travelled in silence for some time. 'It's watered by sub-terranean streams and is the best environment for horses, no matter what they say in California with their wire-fenced enclosures and never a blade of grass in sight!'

Gemma smiled to herself at this defensive outburst.

It was pleasant riding through the wide open spaces. Gradually Gemma felt her guilt and misery at forgetting Rowan's birthday recede from her mind.

'Shade,' she said presently, 'I wanted to talk to you about Todd Ives. I saw him in the garden the other night creeping about near the terraces. What do you suppose he was up to?'

'I shouldn't worry too much about him,' Shade replied, unconcernedly. 'He's okay. Give the man a break!'

'I can't dismiss it as conveniently as that,' said Gemma. 'He's been told not to trespass on Clairmond property. He was there the night of the party too, in the little courtyard . . .'

'Forget it! He's harmless. I'll vouch for him.'

'That's not the point,' persisted Gemma. 'Mrs Prescott would be angry if she knew. She . . . she has a valuable silver collection in the house . . .' She lowered her eyes as she voiced her suspicions.

Shade let out a derisive laugh. 'Todd's not a thief, whatever Mrs Prescott says. Your suggestion is ridiculous.'

'Yes, but he might be considering doing something to the silver to get back at her for . . .' She broke off. It *did* sound ridiculous.

'Not a chance! He's not a thief and he's not a vandal.'

'Then why is she so antagonistic towards him? There's no smoke without fire.'

'Listen, Gemma,' explained Shade patiently. 'Wayne Prescott and Todd's father, Quincey Ives, were partners in a land reclamation scheme in Mexico which went drastically wrong.'

'I know that much. Vikki told me.'

'Well, they were tricked out of a great deal of money,' went on Shade. 'They were both proud men and hated to admit they'd been made a fool of. Each claimed the other was in league with the tricksters, though there was certainly no proof. This scheme was only a sideline for Wayne Prescott and he returned to his tobacco plantations. Quincey Ives, on the other hand, went on to lose money on other projects, proving himself to be a fool as well as a thief, in Wayne's eyes. Mrs Prescott naturally took her husband's side. But Quincey Ives was not dishonest, just weak and foolish. Late in life he took a young bride, but died soon after Todd was born. Todd's had a tough time, but he's an honest man, I swear it.

Please give him a chance.'

Gemma was not too happy about it, but agreed to say nothing to Mrs Prescott, at least for the time being.

They came to a little copse of willows and threaded their way between the trees, over grass peppered with spring flowers.

'Shall we take a breather?' suggested Shade, pulling at the reins and dismounting.

The grey stopped automatically and Gemma considered the daunting prospect of getting down to firm ground.

'Here, slip your feet out of the stirrups and swing your leg over the saddle,' said Shade. 'I'll catch you.'

She followed his instructions and his hands came up to grip her waist. She placed her palms on his forearms and felt the sinews tighten underneath his chequered shirt sleeves. As he set her down in front of him she was conscious of the fact that his hands had slipped up inside her jacket and were resting on her silky blouse, warming her skin in an oddly provocative way. And there was that scent again, strictly male, earthy and piquant.

She laughed awkwardly and made a little movement to draw away from him, but his hands retained their hold upon her. His breathing became shallow and his eyes, when she dared to look, were frankly seductive, half-closed, smouldering.

He moved his hands to her hair and slowly, meticulously removed every pin, allowing the honey-bright tresses to cascade around her shoulders in a shimmering cloud.

'You're so beautiful,' he whispered huskily, pushing his fingers into her hair and gently massaging her scalp.

Gemma sighed and trembled with unexpected pleasure. She saw him moisten his lips and a softening weakness crept through her bloodstream, veiling her mind in a languid haze. She knew he was about to kiss her and was impatient for it to happen. She leaned to-

wards him, her body soft and yielding, drawn by a
mighty tide of emotion that she could not have
resisted—even had she wanted to.

Her arms crept up to wind about his neck and their
bodies moulded together. Slowly, almost reverently, his
lips fastened on hers. It was a tantalising kiss, tender,
with a hint of controlled passion, making no demands
on her, yet awakening her body to a desire she had never
before encountered, moving her to the depths of her
soul. She had felt so low and dejected such a short time
ago, now the caress of this man was like a light at the
end of a long, dark tunnel. Her nerves tingled as he
freed her lips, and her lungs clamoured for air.

His mouth began a journey of exploration, seeking
the pleasure zones behind her ears and in the sensitive
hollows of her throat. She felt his hand slide down to
undo the three buttons of her jacket. He paused, watching her intently, and when she made no protest he moved
to cup the firm fullness of her hardening breasts, his
hands tenderly caressing through the thin material of
her blouse and bra.

Sanity flooded back to her and she gasped. Heavens,
she thought, what was she doing? Standing there giving
every impression of being eager to participate in anything he had in mind! 'Stop it! Let me go!' Panic con-
stricted her throat, making her choke on the words.

Shade ignored her pleas and his fingers found the zip
of the blouse.

'No, no!' she cried, pushing him forcefully from her.

'Don't fight your instincts,' he murmured hoarsely.
'You want me!'

'No!'

Gemma stumbled blindly towards the grey horse and
scrambled into the saddle, her foot feeling desperately
for the farther stirrup.

The startled creature threw up its head and whinnied.
Its eyes became wild and its nostrils flared. As it reared

into the air, Gemma was toppled from her precarious position and slid backwards to land in a crumpled heap on the ground, her leg twisted beneath her. She felt a sharp pain shoot through her ankle and every part of her body seemed to be bruised.

'What did you want to to do a damnfool thing like that for?' demanded Shade, kneeling beside her and cradling her head in his arms. 'Gemma, my dear, are you badly hurt?'

'I don't know,' she moaned. 'I ache all over.'

'It's all my fault,' he said contritely. 'I went too fast.' He gently straightened her leg.

'Just help me up, will you?' she demanded angrily.

'I don't think you'd better stand on that leg,' he replied.

'What do you suggest? That I remain here all day?' She clung to his arm and tried to pull herself up.

'Lie still!' he said authoritatively. 'I'm going to ride back to the farm and get the Range Rover. I shall only be gone a few minutes. If you dare to move while I'm away I'll put you across my knee and spank you!'

She lay back as another stab of pain shot through her ankle. 'All right. But please hurry!'

She watched him swing into the saddle and ride away at great speed. She felt such a fool and cursed herself for acting so childishly, running away like a silly schoolgirl. Behaving so recklessly in the first place. She had intended to be cool and aloof, but had responded to his lovemaking all too readily. If her ankle turned out to be broken it served her right! Once more she wept, but these were tears of self-pity.

CHAPTER SIX

IN hardly any time at all Gemma heard the sound of the Range Rover racing towards her over the uneven ground.

Shade flung himself from the vehicle and ran through the copse to crouch over her. He regarded her trembling lips and her eyes, like misty azure pools. 'You haven't been crying again? You are a funny girl! Everything's going to be okay.'

He picked her up as though she were made of Dresden china and carried her through the slender trees. She noticed that his shirt was damp with perspiration and the veins in his neck stood out. He lifted her into the front seat of the wagon and scrambled in beside her. Gingerly he manoeuvred the vehicle back to the farm, apologising profusely for every bump they encountered along the way.

A babble of anxious voices greeted them as they drove into the yard.

'I've phoned the doctor, boss,' said Todd Ives. 'He's on his way.'

'Thanks, Todd,' said Shade tersely. 'Will you send someone to fetch Fantasy from Fiddler's Copse?'

He carried Gemma up the steps of the house and explained to his mother, who met them in the hall, that Gemma had fallen from her horse. Mrs Lambert opened the door to the sitting-room and watched as Shade lowered Gemma on to the couch, straightened her limbs and placed a scatter cushion behind her head.

'Gee, I'm sorry,' he whispered, smoothing the stray tendrils of hair from her forehead.

'Sorry?' repeated his mother, mystified. 'Was it your fault, Shade?'

106

He grimaced guiltily. 'In a way.'

His mother turned her gaze from his worried face to Gemma's flushed one and summed up the situation. Then she went to the door and called to someone to bring some refreshments.

Gemma felt better after a cup of tea and managed a sheepish grin for Mrs Lambert.

'Where's that doctor?' asked Shade impatiently, striding out into the hall.

They heard him slam the front door and Mrs Lambert seated herself on a chair beside the couch. 'I didn't know you'd gone riding with my son, Gemma.'

'No, it was arranged on the spur of the moment.'

'When I saw Shade carrying someone I thought it must be Elgiva Prescott,' said Mrs Lambert. 'She seems to spend a lot of time in the stables.' The older woman spoke kindly and Gemma perceived she was being warned, in the nicest possible way, not to get carried away by Shade's attentions. So Elgiva came here a lot, did she?

There was the sound of a commotion in the hall and Mrs Lambert rose to her feet. 'Ah, I believe that's the doctor now. I'll leave you alone with him.'

The doctor came breezing into the room, a jolly rotund little man smelling strongly of antiseptics. As he ran his hands expertly over Gemma's bruised frame he asked her what she thought of England's chances in the First Test. She had no idea, but said they were bound to win.

He gave her two sleeping tablets and a painkiller and wrote out a prescription for a further supply of the latter, then he called Shade and his mother in.

'No bones broken, not even a sprain,' he said heartily. 'Take her home and put her to bed. And see that she stays there for a day or two.'

Once more Shade lifted Gemma into his arms and carried her down the steps. She saw with relief that it was the silver-grey Chevrolet which awaited them.

'I've telephoned Mrs Prescott to let her know what's happened,' he told her, switching on the engine. 'I don't think she's too pleased with me.'

Gemma was overcome with a sense of guilt. She was as much to blame as Shade for the accident. She felt she owed him an apology, but nothing would induce her to voice it. Let him stew! she thought.

He drove carefully, but every bump in the road registered on Gemma's aching body. They were met at Clairmond by Mrs Prescott and Vikki.

'You're to go straight to bed,' said the old lady, peering anxiously into Gemma's pallid face as Shade swung her into his arms yet again and started up the steps.

'Please don't fuss,' protested Gemma, disconcerted by the way Shade continued to manhandle her. The sheer bulk of him, coupled with the faint smell of perspiration and aftershave, seemed to smother her, assulting her senses to an overwhelming degree. 'The doctor says I'm only bruised.'

'He ordered a few days' rest,' said Shade sharply, 'so you'll do as you're told.'

The little procession made their way upstairs and presently Shade laid Gemma carefully upon her bed. For a long moment he stood staring down at her. 'I'm sorry,' he said at last.

Gemma noted the knowing glances exchanged between Mrs Prescott and Vikki and wished he wouldn't keep saying that. It conveyed to the others that something had happened.

'I was as much to blame as you!' she admitted sleepily, feeling the tablets beginning to work.

His eyes flickered to the bedside table where Rowan's photograph stood. He examined it briefly and a smile twisted wryly about his mouth. Then he bade them all good day and left the bedroom.

The memory of his kisses remained with Gemma in

the darkened room, and when she finally drifted off to sleep his face returned to bewitch her dreams.

Gemma opened her eyes and stared at her bedroom ceiling, then around at her little clock. Nine-fifteen and the sun was shining round the edges of the curtains. She must have slept the rest of the day and all through the night.

She moved warily and was relieved to find that her ankle did not throb any more. Throwing back the duvet and examining her body, she saw that the bruises were not as bad as she had feared.

Vikki came in with a tray from which emanated the appetising smell of coffee and hot rolls.

'Think you can sit up?' she asked.

Gemma eased herself into a sitting position while Vikki thumped up the pillows.

'You're spoiling me!' exclaimed Gemma, looking at the little pots of butter, honey, syrup and jam.

'Enjoy it while you can,' said Vikki. 'Mrs Prescott's orders are that you're to stay in bed.'

'Oh, I can't . . .'

'There's no harm in taking things easy once in a while,' grinned the housekeeper. 'Spring can be hectic in our calendar. There's the pageant only six days away, then the trip to the cottage in Buffalo at Whitsun.' She paused and eyed Gemma speculatively. 'What did happen between you and Shade yesterday? I've never seen you with your hair down before.'

Gemma blushed but declined to answer.

'He's been ringing since seven this morning to find out how you are,' went on Vikki. 'You sure gave him a scare—and serve him right. It sounds very much like he tried to seduce you and you fled his amorous advances!'

'Something like that!' admitted Gemma, unable to hide a grin at Vikki's dramatic choice of words.

'Gee, you'd think he had enough women chasing after

him without having to use force on the unwilling ones,'
sighed Vikki.

'He sees me as a challenge,' said Gemma. 'He said as
much the day after I arrived.'

'Well, carry on resisting him,' advised Vikki. 'Men
like that care only for the conquest, not for the responsibility of involvement. Once you've surrendered
he'll cast you aside like yesterday's newspaper.'

'Don't worry,' said Gemma, 'I'm not about to surrender to anyone, least of all to Shade Lambert.'

After Vikki had gone, Gemma pondered the events of
the previous day, coming to the conclusion that Shade
had taken an unfair advantage of her. She had been so
possessed with thoughts of Rowan and the futility of it
all that Shade—a comparative stranger offering comfort—had been able to steal up and catch her unawares,
laying all her plans for resisting him to waste.

She had not warmed to such desire for many a long
day, and the fulfilment of it had momentarily become
the most important thing in the world. 'You want me,'
he had said, and for an instant it had been true. A
memory of past loving had been kindled, a longing for
what might have been. And now it was possible to believe that she might fall in love again—one day.

It was difficult to visualise, but if it did happen then
it would not, must not, be with someone like Shade
Lambert—he who loved and left with equanimity!

If she surrendered herself to him then only heartbreak
would follow and she would be even worse off.

She and Rowan had shared a wonderful love and she
couldn't risk soiling his memory. It had been the real
thing. Whatever Shade could offer, however splendid, it
could only be transitory.

The children's pageant, illustrating American history in
general, and Kentucky history in particular, was to be
performed on the emerald lawns of Clairmond, and

during the next six days Gemma's time was fully occupied with all the administration worries.

She had not seen Shade since the day of the accident, although he had telephoned to ask how she was and to say that he was too busy with foaling to call round. Gemma had snapped his head off as usual and reflected to herself that he was not too busy to take Elgiva out, for that brazen miss had boasted of going to the theatre with him on two occasions.

The teachers of the three schools involved with the pageant had been busy rehearsing the hundred or so children taking part; the parents had made the costumes and scenery; and Gemma was responsible for all the mundane tasks like hiring three hundred fold-up chairs and a marquee, taking out insurance cover, sending invitations to the V.I.P. guests, arranging for the electronic equipment to be set up, and issuing instructions to the gardener to cut the vast areas of grass around the summerhouse.

The children would be bringing packed lunches, but the important guests were to lunch in the marquee, so Gemma was required to liaise with Vikki over the catering preparations.

Pageants came easy to Gemma, for she had helped out with several at the school in Buckinghamshire, although she had to admit that American history was an unknown quantity as far as she was concerned.

'I do hope it's a fine day,' said Vikki, watching the staff of Clairmond running about with chairs and plates. 'It will be a pity if everyone gets a soaking.'

Rain or fine, the event was scheduled to start at ten o'clock on May Day morning, and by nine the cars and buses were streaming along the drive under a clear blue sky. The spectators' chairs were set against a backdrop of fir trees where flocks of crested cardinals, Kentucky's state birds, perched like red flowers amidst the dark greenery. Nearby stood the onion-domed summerhouse, its gilded tiles gleaming in the sun, its white marbled colonnades smothered with climbing roses. It was on the steps of this building that the senior percussion band and junior school choir had taken up their positions. The whole scene was reflected in the still water of an oval-shaped lake.

One of the teachers welcomed the audience, then began to read from the script as the first colourful procession moved from its hiding place among the trees and crossed the lawn. When the children reached the edge of the lake they paused to form a tableau to illustrate the arrival of the Spanish conquistadors with their leader, Fernando de Soto, complete with sword and false beard.

Gemma had been elected to read the next item, and as a little knot of children, richly dressed as Elizabethans, tripped over the lawn to pose beside the lake, she took her place at the microphone. She relayed Queen Elizabeth's greeting to Sir Francis Drake as he arrived in a cardboard cut-out *Golden Hind* laden with Spanish gold, then wished god-speed to Sir Walter Raleigh as he set sail for America.

Gemma stayed to describe the arrival of the Pilgrim Fathers, a handful of sombrely-dressed Puritans weary after their three-thousand-mile journey across the Atlantic, then she stepped down from the dais. As she did so she was surprised to observe Shade standing behind the back row of chairs. How long he had been there she had no idea.

While warpainted Indians whooped and danced across the lawns, Gemma found a seat on the steps of the summerhouse and· a moment later was joined by Shade.

He gave her an arrogantly appraising look. 'You slayed 'em with your English accent!'

She ignored him and concentrated on the children who were re-enacting the Boston Massacre.

'Don't take it to heart,' whispered Shade, seeing her frown. 'We've forgiven the British now.'

'Huh!' she hissed. 'It was hardly a massacre! Three men shot at the hands of panicky soldiers!'

Next came the Boston Tea-Party, another blow to Gemma's patriotic pride, and she gritted her teeth as the Bostonians, disguised as Mohawk Indians, crept aboard the plywood ships to dump crates of tea into the harbour.

The War of Independence was of special interest to the onlookers, for the first shots were fired right here in Lexington. There were tableaux of the Minute Men, the Green Mountain Boys, the Battle of Bunker's Hill and Paul Revere's midnight ride to warn the people of Concord that the 'bloody British' were coming. Lord Cornwallis surrendered to George Washington; the latter was inaugurated as the first president; then it was time for lunch.

'I must go and see if Vikki wants any help,' said Gemma, rising and dusting the seat of her black skirt.

'Don't be too long, then,' said Shade. 'I want to speak to you.'

She tossed her head. 'I'm far too busy . . .'

'Dammit, Gemma, if you're not out of that marquee in fifteen minutes, I'll come and drag you out!' he countered.

Gemma took a deep breath and slowly expelled it before turning away. She made her way to the marquee where Mrs Prescott introduced her to a number of distinguished guests, including a Congressman and his wife. Gemma helped serve the hors d'oeuvres and managed to eat a chicken sandwich, then caught sight of Shade standing in the entrance of the tent. Recalling his threat, she hastily moved towards him.

As they stepped into the sunshine his hand gripped her elbow and he propelled her towards a little path leading to the rear of the summerhouse. 'I can't stay for the rest of the show—I have two mares about to foal. I only came to witness your Queen Elizabeth speeches. You did well.'

'Thank you,' she smiled, assuming that Mrs Prescott had told him of her part in it. 'It's going very smoothly isn't it? The children are so well behaved.'

'It's their Southern upbringing,' said Shade proudly. 'The old-fashioned courtesy, you know.'

'So that's what it is,' she mocked him. 'I hadn't realised.'

'Okay, so you haven't received much Southern chivalry from me!' he grinned. 'I owe you an apology for my brutish behaviour the other day.'

'Oh, don't let's go into all that again,' she sighed wearily. 'It's over and done with as far as I'm concerned.'

'I want to make it up to you,' he said, ignoring her protest, 'to show you I do know how to behave.'

She selfconsciously smoothed the wide lace cuffs of her white blouse. 'There's no need, I assure you.'

'I'd like to take you to the races in Louisville,' Shade went on. 'It's Derby Day the first Saturday in May.'

'The Kentucky Derby?' Her breath caught in her throat and her eyes shone.

'Sure thing! Well, what do you say? Will you come with me?'

'Mrs Prescott . . .'

'. . . Says it's okay,' he finished.

'I wish you wouldn't present me with a *fait accompli*,' Gemma said irritably.

'Gemma!' His fingers increased their pressure on her arm. 'Will you allow me to take you to the Kentucky Derby?'

'I don't know,' she said slowly, giving a negligent shrug of her shoulders, and relishing his expression of impatience. She intended to let him wait for her answer. 'I don't want another twisted ankle.'

'That's not fair,' he chided her. 'You said the incident was forgotten. Are you going to throw it in my face every time it suits you?'

She moistened her dry lips with the tip of her tongue. 'Probably.'

His eyes focussed on her mouth. 'How like a woman!'

'You're the expert!'

'Give me a chance to make up for the twisted ankle, then,' he said urgently. 'You'll enjoy it, I promise. Derby Day is an unforgettable experience. The Kentucky Derby is acknowledged to be the most exciting two minutes in the world of sport. How can you afford to pass it up?'

She squinted up at him slyly. 'What about Elgiva? She's been, many times.'

'That's not what I meant and you know it! What will she think of your taking me out?'

'It has nothing to do with Elgiva,' he said, a note of exasperation creeping into his voice. 'She doesn't own me.'

'That's not the impression I get.'

Shade shook his head and chuckled. 'I don't know what she's been saying, but you've gotten the wrong idea about Elgiva and me.'

Gemma fiddled with her sleeves again, recalling her resolve to stay clear of him. But she was mightily tempted, and little tremors were running up and down her backbone at the thought of spending some time with him. Where was the harm . . . if she kept her head . . .?

'If it makes you feel any better, I'll promise not to lay a finger on you!' he interrupted her thoughts, a crooked grin tugging at his lips.

She hid a smile. 'In that case, how can I refuse? Thanks, I'd love to come.'

He slapped her on the back. 'That's great!'

Gemma noticed the audience returning to their seats and said hurriedly, 'I must be getting back.'

He ran his fingertip gently under her chin. 'See yo
Saturday. I'll pick you up at noon.'

Gemma found a seat next to Mrs Prescott to watc
the rest of the pageant. This part concerned the story c
the local frontiersman, Daniel Boone, and was close t
the heart of every Kentuckian. It was Boone who pene
trated Cumberland Gap and explored Kentucky, open
ing the way for the early settlers.

Listening to the applause, Gemma was struck by th
depth of feelings the people had for their state, seein
themselves as Kentuckians rather than Americans.

During the enactment of the Civil War, the choir san
'Marching through Georgia' to accompany the arriv
of General Grant's Northern army, and 'Dixie' fo
General Lee's Southern rebels.

'Kentucky was a border state between the two sides
explained Mrs Prescott. 'They were divided, neighbou
against neighbour, resulting in many casualties.'

The pageant finished with a line-up of generals, a
tronauts and presidents, and the audience rose to its fee
in tumultuous applause. The Congressman said a fe
words, Mrs Prescott was called to be thanked, an
everyone gradually drifted away.

'All over save the clearing up,' sighed Vikki, lookin
at the scene of devastation in and around the marque

'You decided to go to the Derby with Shade, then'
asked Mrs Prescott, her thinly-sketched brows raise
enquiringly, when the family met for dinner that eve
ing.

Gemma shot a wary glance across the table in Elgiva
direction. 'Why, yes,' she replied brightly. 'I've alway
wanted to see that famous race. My sister will be gree
with envy.'

Elgiva grinned but said nothing. She wore a startlin
black jump-suit with white piping, which fitted so snug
it could have been sprayed on. Her long hair was pile

on top of her head and she wore high-heeled cowboy boots. She was obviously going out after the meal, thought Gemma.

'The Kentucky Derby is the first leg in the American Triple Crown,' said Judge Dean, who had joined them for dinner. 'It's the greatest classic race for three-year-olds in this country and a supreme test for a thoroughbred. Shade is the perfect escort for this event because he's an expert on bloodstock.'

Elgiva spoke at last. 'Fancy him, do you?' she taunted softly.

'Who?' asked Gemma, concentrating on her filet mignon.

Elgiva gave a little laugh, a brittle sound that grated on Gemma's ears.

'She means Shade,' said Mrs Prescott. 'She always means Shade these days.'

Elgiva looked Gemma straight in the eye. 'Has it occurred to you that Shade might have asked me first to go to the Derby with him?' she asked silkily. 'And that I declined the invitation?'

Gemma felt her cheeks growing warm. That thought had not occurred to her.

'That's highly unlikely,' said Mrs Prescott. 'You'd have gone like a shot.'

'Oh, would I?' asked Elgiva, glaring at her grandmother. 'I like to play hard to get sometimes.'

Mrs Prescott almost choked over her wine. 'You?'

'Oh, be quiet, Gran,' grinned Elgiva. She toyed with a silver spoon, then smiled across at Gemma again. 'I hope you have a nice day,' she crooned. 'Make the most of it, dear. You may be surprised to hear it, but I don't see you as a threat. Shade's attracted to you for the moment, because you're so cold and indifferent towards him, but the novelty will wear off and he'll realise he needs a woman of flesh and blood. I can wait until he gets you out of his system.'

'Elgiva!' admonished Mrs Prescott. 'How dare yo
speak to Gemma like that! Apologise or leave th
table!'

'I've finished anyway,' said Elgiva, rising languidl
'But I'll apologise all the same. Sorry, Gemma, I real
am. But you know I'm right.'

'Funny kind of apology,' observed Judge Dean.

Churchill Downs was packed to capacity for th
Kentucky Derby. Gemma had never been to a big rad
meeting and the thrill of being there in the thick of
was unlike anything she had ever experienced.

'Anything goes as far as clothes are concerned,' Vik
had told her helpfully, 'but I should wear somethir
chic and simple if I were you. Shade's a respected ma
in local horse circles and he's bound to have a pass int
the V.I.P. lounge.'

The two of them had combed through Gemma's ne
wardrobe and come up with a sunray-pleated primro
dress teamed with a white boxy jacket. Gemma still fe
undressed without the jade pendant and she added
large azure brooch which complemented her eyes. Sl
was pleased with the image of the girl gazing back
her from the bedroom mirror, so cool and feminin
belying the nervous churning in her stomach at th
prospect of spending the afternoon with Shade.

She watched from the window as he drove up
Clairmond in the sleek black Porsche. He was formal
dressed in a light grey suit with matching waistcoat ar
a gold watch chain slung across his chest, and Gemn
noted how gracefully he climbed out of the low-slu
car. As she opened the front door to him his silent a
praisal was reward enough for all the trouble she ha
taken in dressing.

It took just under an hour to drive to Louisville ar
Shade talked the whole time, filling her in with deta
of previous Derby winners. He brimmed with confiden

at she was going to bring him luck.

'Are you a gambling man?' she asked.

'Heck, no! I haven't the time. But the Kentucky Derby kinda special. Everyone has a flutter.'

The racecourse was in the centre of the city and the ain stand was immense, with attractive Victorian ires on its roof.

'Anything goes', Vikki had said. There were girls in ivenchy dresses rubbing shoulders with jean-clad ppies and raucous cowboy types. Gemma had xpected to see bookmakers and tic-tac men and was ightly disappointed.

'Only the totalisator is legal now,' said Shade, tucking er arm through his so that they would not get separated they pushed through the tightly packed throng. 'Back 1875 when it all began it was a different story. I have pass to the V.I.P. lounge and tickets for lunch,' he ent on. 'Would you like to go?'

Gemma nodded, 'Yes, please.'

They were met at the door by a benign-looking ntleman in a black tuxedo and an upper-crust mat- arch who subjected Gemma to a thorough scrutiny, s X-ray eyes mentally tallying the labels and price tags n every item of her clothing. The glance only took ten conds, but it succeeded in making Gemma feel thank- l indeed for Mrs Prescott's charge account.

'Was that some kind of entrance test?' she whispered hen they were issued with badges and ushered into the allowed precincts. 'I feel I've been stripped.'

Shade squeezed her arm. 'You'd get in wearing a flour ck. You've got class written all over you.'

Gemma basked in the warmth of his compliment.

There was an aura of wealth and prosperity in the unge. A long buffet table was spread with such de- acies as Beluga caviare, pâté de foie gras and ripe ilton. A white-hatted chef was employed solely for the rpose of carving the Nova Scotia salmon and two

waiters were busy serving the chilled Veuve Clicquot
crystal glasses.

'Shade, sugarpie!' A young woman, quite plainly o
of the top drawer of American society, bore down
him. 'Long time no see! You promised to phone
after your London trip, but you never did!'

He dropped a kiss on her cheek and mumbled so
excuse about being busy. Later two more wom
accosted him, demanding to know where he'd been sin
Christmas. Gemma wondered idly what had kept h
from them. Not Elgiva, for she had only just return
home.

He seemed completely at home in this setting and
female eyes were upon him as he moved easily abo
the room comparing notes on the race with 'those in
know'.

They partook of the food and drink, then Shade
Gemma outside again to see the horses parading in
paddock.

'Right,' he said at last, 'I think we're ready to pl
our bets now. Are you willing to rely on my judgmer

'Oh yes.'

They climbed the steps to the tote pay grilles a
Gemma saw Shade hand over a hefty wad of notes.

'I thought I'd just risk ten dollars,' she said. S
placed the tickets carefully in her handbag and allow
Shade to propel her towards the front of the main sta
overlooking the dirt track.

A hush fell over the gigantic crowd and Gemma
Shade grow tense beside her. Then, to her amazem
and delight, the air was filled with the melodious sou
of a hundred thousand voices singing 'My Old Kentu
Home'. Shade's voice, close to her ear, sounded ple
antly deep and tuneful.

All these well-heeled gentlefolk singing about li
cabin floors and hard times a-coming made Gem
want to laugh, but she recognised the folly of giving

to such an urge and held her amusement in check. As they came to the line 'Weep no more, my lady' she glanced about her, to see grown men with tears in their eyes.

'Another tradition?' she asked Shade sardonically when the song had died away.

'That song is by the famous son of Kentucky, Stephen Foster,' he answered, his voice husky with emotion. 'It never fails to reduce the toughest Kentuckian to tears.'

The stall-gates on the track sprang open and the horses made a dash forward to secure a good position on the first bend and produce further bursts of speed on the straight—an indispensable attribute of the successful racehorse, Shade told Gemma, bringing his binoculars into play to follow the field.

'They run for a mile and a quarter,' he continued. 'The ideal horse is able to start quickly and maintain a fast pace for that limited distance.'

It really was an exciting two minutes, Gemma acknowledged, as the crowd roared and cheered.

All of a sudden Shade threw his arms about Gemma and her breath was knocked out of her lungs as he swung her round.

'Have we won?' she asked.

'I'll say we have! Three to one!'

'Three to one?' she repeated. 'Why, that's thirty dollars I've won. We did back it to win?'

'We sure did, baby!'

They stayed until the end of the meeting, backing three more winners and two losers. There was a three-mile queue of cars out of the track and, when they finally got clear, Shade drove along by the Ohio river.

'I thought you might like to catch a glimpse of the *Belle of Louisville*. It's due to dock any moment now.'

They parked in the Riverfront Plaza Garage and walked to the wharf. The sight took Gemma's breath away. It was a paddle-powered, flag-strewn honey of a steamboat, with crowds of people lining its three decks. As it docked its mellow whistle played 'Sweet Georgia Brown'.

Shade stood close behind Gemma, his arms encircling her body so that his hands rested on the wharf rails. Every time he spoke his breath fanned the top of her head, sending little tingles along her scalp and sharpening her awareness of his virile proximity.

'Care for a drink?' he asked, cocking his head in the direction of a riverside bar.

'Can I have a cup of tea?' she asked, when they were inside.

'Good idea,' agreed Shade. 'I need to remember I'm driving.' He gazed at her with that frankly sensual look which seemed to come so easily to his eyes. 'Besides, the nearness of you is intoxicating enough for me.'

She looked away quickly, overcome with embarrassment. Moments earlier she had been thinking the same thing about him.

It was a self-service bar and Shade went to order while Gemma found a couple of satin-covered armchairs. Presently he placed two cups of tea on the table, his black with a slice of lemon, hers milky. He absently unwrapped the three sugar lumps he had brought for her and dropped them into her cup.

She wrinkled her brow. 'How do you know I take three?'

He smiled broadly. 'I know everything about you.'

She fixed her eyes on his elegantly knotted tie. 'I hope not!'

She laid her head against the scarlet seat, such a contrast to her fair hair and colouring, and the light clothes she wore, that it emphasised her cool serenity.

'You're beautiful!' Shade told her.

'What brought that on?' she asked, disconcerted, but he declined to answer.

He took out his gold watch and perused it thoughtfully. 'Shall we eat Kentuckian this evening? I know a swell place this side of Lexington. What do you say?'

'I'd like that, but we mustn't be too late.'

'You can lie in tomorrow,' he reasoned. 'It's Sunday.'

'No, I can't. We're all off to Buffalo on Wednesday and I still have a lot of preparation to do.'

'I promise you'll be home and tucked up in your bed before midnight,' he grinned.

CHAPTER SEVEN

THEY travelled the freeway for some miles then, as dusk was falling, turned off into a secondary road until they were deep into the heart of a wooded countryside. The car swung into a leafy lane, then the trees thinned to reveal a large ivy-clad log cabin overlooking a winding river.

Hidden in the country it might be, thought Gemma, but the cars crowding the forecourt were evidence of the restaurant's popularity. They entered a low-ceilinged room with the look of an old trading post about it. The walls were covered with pelts and ancient rifles, and the furniture seemed to be fashioned from gunpowder kegs. A barber shop quartet occupied a small stage and was giving a soft melodious rendition of 'Sweet Adeline'.

A black-coated head waiter led the way to a candlelit booth next to a window overlooking the floodlit river, where swans were settling for the night in the water weeds.

Despite the downbeat look of the place, Gemma suspected that it was very expensive, and one glance at the menu card proved her right.

'What would you like to eat?' enquired Shade, sitting opposite her and smiling indulgently. 'This place is renowned for real Kentucky cooking.'

'In that case I leave the choice to the expert,' she smiled, handing him her menu.

They began with clam chowder, which turned out to be a highly flavoured fish soup. The waiter uncorked the Château Haut-Brion and Shade asked Gemma if she had enjoyed her day out.

'Enormously,' she enthused, watching him sniff the dark wine, then roll it expertly around his tongue. 'My sister is never going to believe I backed the winner of the Kentucky Derby.'

The country ham and fried corn arrived and Shade said, 'I haven't eaten here for months. I'd almost forgotten how good the food is.'

'Hm! It's delicious,' said Gemma after a forkful of the succulent ham, wondering who he had brought here the last time.

'You mentioned your sister,' said Shade. 'Do you miss the folks back home?'

'In a way,' replied Gemma, twirling the stem of her glass and seeing the candlelight catch the crimson contents. 'But Mrs Prescott is such a slave-driver I don't have much time to get homesick. Have you any brothers and sisters?'

'No, I'm an only child,' he said. 'My father died in a riding accident when I was four, so I've always been the man of the house.'

She tried to picture him as a child, then a lanky teenager growing fast into a man, but it was difficult to see him in the agonies of adolescence, starting to shave and becoming aware of the opposite sex. 'You must be a tower of strength to your mother,' she mused.

'I suppose so.' A reflective look glazed his eyes. 'Of course, she had a manager for the farm while I was growing up and away at 'varsity, but it was always a foregone conclusion that I would take over eventually. Horses are in my blood.'

'University?' she prompted.

'I'm a Harvard man.' He sounded inordinately proud.

'I might have known! The cream of universities.'

'I majored in biological sciences and mathematics,' he threw in.

'I'm impressed. But horses are your great love.'

He gazed at her from half-closed eyes. 'One of them!' The waiter brought two portions of jam cake smothered with cream and the barber shop quartet was replaced by a man wearing scruffy jeans and a straw boater, carrying a violin.

'That's Casey Greencheese,' said Shade. 'He's a wizard at authentic old-time fiddling.'

The air was filled with the frantic strains of the music and all conversation was suspended until he had worked through his repertoire. Gemma was exhilarated by the foot-tapping sound and she clapped until her hands were sore.

'I'm so glad you liked it,' said Shade. 'It was one of the reasons I brought you here.' He refilled their glasses. 'Two of these must be my limit as I'm driving. I can't take risks with such a precious cargo.'

He really was being most charming, thought Gemma.

'But don't let me stop you,' he urged.

'Oh no, I'm not a great drinker. I'm apt to act a bit wildly if I have more than two glasses.'

'I've noticed.' He asked the waiter for a cigar and lit up, leaning back contentedly in his chair.

'I didn't know you smoked,' said Gemma.

'I don't as a rule. I gave it up years ago because smoking's a dangerous habit on a horse farm. But this is a special occasion.'

A movement beyond the window caught Gemma's eye and she turned her head to watch the swans squabbling over the best resting places.

'You'd think the floodlights would disturb them,' commented Shade.

'I remember thinking the same thing when I saw swans in similar surroundings outside a floodlit hotel window in Salisbury on the river Avon,' said Gemma nostalgically, 'but they seemed to revel in the light.'

'You went there with Rowan, I presume?' he asked softly, a faint challenge in his tone.

'Yes. He was doing part of his medical training at a hospital there and I went down for the weekend to stay at the Rose and Crown. It's an old coaching inn and I slept in a four-poster bed . . .'

'Alone?'

She met his eyes levelly and said, without ire, 'It's none of your business.'

He shrugged indifferently. 'Your choice of the *singular* first person pronoun told me all I needed to know.'

There was a long pause, then he said, 'You're right, it's none of my business. I'm sorry.'

His apology was so unexpected that she was taken aback. She carefully lined up the unused cutlery on the table. 'We were so happy then.'

'Such memories!' he said with a slight edge to his voice. 'Were there no unhappy ones?'

'No!'

'It was all moonlight and lollipops, was it?' He leaned forward across the table. 'I can't accept that. I've always been under the impression that the real thing hurts.'

'You would be!' she retorted mildly. Oh, how had they managed to get on this subject again? 'I know you think I view love through rose-coloured spectacles, but you go too far in the other direction. Millions of people fall in love, get married and live happily ever after.'

Shade's explosive laugh sent the candle flames dancing. 'My dear girl, how naïve you are! Marriage has nothing to do with it. Right now one of my uncles is going through his fourth divorce, would you believe? Enough of my friends and relations have split up for me to be very wary.'

'But if you were really in love . . . I mean *really* in love, so much that you couldn't visualise the future without the other person . . .'

He raked his fingers through his dark hair. 'I don't believe such a love is possible.' He was silent for a long moment, then he asked quietly, 'How did Rowan die?'

'He was a hard-pressed medical student, working in Casualty . . . he was killed on his motorcycle . . . He'd

just finished the night shift ... the road was wet ...'
Gemma managed to keep her voice steady, but her eyes
smarted with unshed tears and there was an aching lump
in her throat.

'Did you see him before he died?'

'Yes, he lived two days after the accident,' she whispered. 'I was with him at the end.'

'And he exacted a promise from you to stay faithful?'
asked Shade bluntly.

'No! No!' she answered impatiently. 'He told me to
forget him and find someone else. But I don't want to.'

Shade called for the bill. 'I brought you out today to
give you a good time, not to provoke you into our familiar argument. Shall we drop the subject?'

He helped her on with her jacket and, as his hands
lingered on her shoulders, Gemma trembled suddenly.
He had behaved very courteously, but now the day was
coming to a close. Would he spoil everything by trying
to kiss her goodnight—or more? She prayed they
wouldn't have a fight at Clairmond's front door!

She was feeling tired now and yawned as she slid into
the front seat of the Porsche. Shade watched her in the
light from the roof bulb before he slammed the door
and they were plunged into darkness. 'You're always
lovely,' he said quietly. 'So aloof and poised, so independent. But when you're relaxed, as you are now, you
positively glow!' He started the engine and placed his
hands on the steering wheel.

She smiled to herself and, leaning back, closed her
eyes.

As they reached the main road she heard him say, 'I
wish I hadn't made that silly promise.'

'What promise?' she murmured sleepily.

'Not to lay a finger on you!'

She opened her eyes and stared, instantly alert,
thankful that he could not witness the sudden rush of
blood to her cheeks. His profile was outlined, firm and

strong, against the lights of the freeway outside. Her heart gave a little lurch of pleasure just looking at him. She had enjoyed being squired by him more than she had ever imagined possible, and she had witnessed a new gentle side of the man that she had not suspected existed.

It began to rain, and the steady purr of the windscreen wipers lulled Gemma to sleep. Almost at once she felt Shade gently shaking her arm, and looked up to see the stately portals of Clairmond. 'Come on, sleepyhead, you're home.'

They ran through the rain, up the steps to the porch. As Gemma fumbled with the door catch, Shade restrained her.

'I shan't come in,' he said.

She was relieved. Or was she? He stood very close to her and his fingers were tightly clasped around her wrist. She felt her body tremble violently. 'Why? Scared of meeting Elgiva?' she asked flippantly, for something to say.

He moved his arms to encircle her shoulders. 'I can handle that one!'

Gemma's breath shuddered treacherously in her throat and she realised she wanted him to kiss her, longed to lose herself in his embrace. She turned to him quickly. 'Thank you for a wonderful time, Shade. I enjoyed every moment of it.' She gazed up at his face, illuminated by the light from above the door.

'Yes, we get on well together when we're not trying to score off one another, don't we?' His fingers caressed her shoulder blades. 'I think we can be friends after all.'

He was watching her lips and she parted them expectantly, willing him to claim them. What was he waiting for?

'Dammit, Gemma, I'd like nothing better than to stay and make love to you,' the amusement in his voice was unmistakable, 'but I must maintain my rôle of the

Southern gentleman.' He lowered his face to hers and feathered her cheek with his lips. 'Goodnight, honey.'

As he turned on his heel and retreated down the steps, she experienced a faint stab of vexation. How dared he! she thought. He had reduced her to a mass of longing, then walked away!

Taking a deep breath to establish her composure, she entered the house and leaned heavily against the door.

'We can be friends', he had said. Oh no, she thought wildly, they could not be friends. Lovers, maybe. But not friends!

On the Wednesday before Whitsun, Gemma accompanied Mrs Prescott north to Buffalo city in the private plane, a sturdy Piper Cherokee, piloted by Yarwood.

Elgiva had been expected to accompany them, but had cried off at the last moment, saying she wanted to spend the holiday with some friends from the secretarial college.

Gemma had digested this information with scepticism, deciding that Elgiva had elected to stay behind in order to see more of Shade.

Gemma had done a good deal of heart-searching since she had seen him last. He had tried to seduce her during their horse ride, then, in complete contrast, had behaved coolly on Derby Day. She began to suspect that this treatment was part of a carefully calculated plan—to arouse her interest, then stand back while frustration set in and she dropped like a ripe apple. Well, it wasn't going to work! She had come very near to falling under his spell, but she wasn't after a quick affair, which was all he was likely to offer. She had suffered enough pain over Rowan's death; why lay herself open to more? With this reasoning in mind she was really looking forward to these ten days away from Lexington and Shade Lambert. She needed time to think without having to block his advances all the time.

Everyone had spoken so casually of the 'cottage' in Buffalo that she had fully expected to see a pretty little house with honeysuckle round the door. In fact she had first mistaken the lodge, just inside the gates, for the cottage itself. She was suitably impressed, therefore, to find that their destination was a low rambling ten-bedroomed house. It had clearly started out as a bungalow, then several rooms had been added in the roof, as indicated by the dormer windows set in the blue tiles. It was situated in an exclusive area beside Lake Erie just outside Buffalo city, its verdant lawns sweeping down to the water's edge.

Two retainers, Mr and Mrs Judd, lived permanently at the lodge and looked after the cottage. However, Vikki had motored up in the Cadillac a few days before the others to make final arrangements and engage some extra local staff from an agency for the duration of the holiday.

The house was furnished throughout in nineteenth-century style. In the drawing-room the tangerine damask curtains were drawn back from the tall latticed windows to afford an uninterrupted view of the lake, dotted with the coloured sails of hundreds of yachts.

The dining-room was vast and formal. The rectangular mahogany table had ten Sheraton chairs with plush velvet seats placed on either side of its length and carver chairs at head and foot. Sliding glass doors led out to a paved patio containing wrought-iron garden furniture.

Gemma's bedroom was one of those built into the roof, with a sloping ceiling and pretty traditional drapes. She was thrilled to discover that the bed had tall walnut posts like those she had seen in old movies.

Mrs Prescott invited a few of the neighbours in for dinner that first evening, people she had known for years. Gemma noticed how at ease her employer was in this beautiful setting. She obviously loved the house and was probably reminded of past holidays with her husband.

After dinner Gemma played bridge with the others and acquitted herself well, despite not having played for several years.

Next day the weather turned very warm and Gemma donned halter top and shorts to join Mrs Prescott on the deck of her cabin cruiser which was moored permanently at the lake. The two ladies sunned themselves in lounger chairs while Yarwood, who was turning out to be a man of many talents, handled the craft with expertise.

The water sparkled in the sunshine and there was a balmy breeze blowing across the lake. By the end of the morning, Gemma was pleased to see she was getting a nice even tan.

'Over there,' said Mrs Prescott, pointing vaguely at the far horizon, 'is Canada.'

'Isn't Niagara Falls in that direction?' asked Gemma, shielding her eyes, but seeing nothing but water.

'Yes. When Judge Dean arrives I'll ask him to take you there one day, dear. I won't come, though. It's a bit too strenuous for me.'

Mrs Prescott was in a state of excitement during dinner that evening because Judge Dean was expected any moment and she needed him there to make the vacation complete. He had rung earlier in the day to say he was bringing a friend with him and the staff had been busy getting one of the upstairs rooms ready for the extra guest.

Dinner was over by the time the message was relayed over the house phone from the lodge that the Judge's cab was driving in the gates.

The lights from the cab swept over the sliding glass doors and moments later Bradley Dean entered with— Shade!

'How wonderful!' exclaimed Mrs Prescott, taking

both men's arms and receiving their kisses on her cheeks.
'My two favourite guys. But why the mystery? Why
didn't you let us know you were the surprise guest,
Shade?'

'Then it would be no surprise.' His eyes sought out
Gemma sitting at the table finishing her coffee.

'Have you eaten?' asked Mrs Prescott, pulling on the
service rope beside the deep stone fireplace.

'Yes, we snatched something on the plane,' said
Shade. 'We didn't want to put you to too much
trouble.'

'Whenever has entertaining you two been any
trouble?' asked Mrs Prescott indignantly. 'At least you'll
have coffee and liqueurs?'

'We will,' said the Judge, seating himself at the table
and lighting a cigar.

'Hi, Gemma, how was your day?' Shade asked
amiably, taking a chair opposite her and reaching for
the coffee pot.

His gaze was so intent she could almost feel it touch
her skin and she experienced those familiar goose
pimples breaking out over her flesh.

'Fine.' She stared down at the lace tablecloth. She
was at a loss for words at his unexpected appearance. It
was going to be difficult to ignore him while they were
both under the same roof. She wondered why he had
decided to come to Buffalo. Had he fallen out with
Elgiva? The girl had obviously set great store by spending this vacation with him, and yet he was here. Gemma
was intrigued.

The four of them played bridge into the small hours,
with Gemma and Shade partnered against Mrs Prescott
and the Judge. Gemma caught a glimpse of Shade's
devious mind as they won rubber after rubber, despite
her own mediocre playing.

Shade's sudden arrival had made her nervous and she
continued to let him down, allowing tricks to go by and

failing to take the lead. At one point he reached across the table and took her wrist in a lazy grip. 'It would help, honey, if you didn't trump my aces!'

'You played extremely badly, Gemma,' said Mrs Prescott peevishly when they had finished and were enjoying a last drink.

Shade stretched out his long legs. 'We won, nevertheless.' He tilted his chair back at a reckless angle, arrogantly defying the law of gravity, and gazed out of the window at the moonlit lake.

While he was thus preoccupied, Gemma treated herself to the pleasure of studying the superb length of him, noting his aggressive jawline, the way his well-cut slacks emphasised his lean hips, how the casual shirt strained at the seams as he raised his arm to push his fingers through his dense hair. When he turned his head towards her again there was a look of cool amusement in his eyes and she realised that he had been watching her reflection in the window and was aware of her interest.

'You reprimanded me when I looked at you like that,' he whispered so that only she could hear.

She had a strong urge to kick the chair from under him. Instead she affected a yawn and excused herself with all possible speed.

Shade's room was quite near to Gemma's on the first floor, and as she emerged the next morning she saw him closing his door. She wondered if he had been watching out for her.

He wore a navy sports shirt and white shorts exposing very brown legs.

'Anything planned for the day?' he asked, following her down the stairs.

'I expect Mrs Prescott has plenty of letters for me to type . . .' began Gemma.

'Holy cow! She doesn't expect you to work while you're on holiday, does she?' he exclaimed.

'I'm not on holiday,' insisted Gemma. 'I'm still at work. And we've brought the typewriter with us.'

'You haven't any letters you want typing, have you, Henrietta?' asked Shade, marching through the dining-room and out on to the patio where the others were already breakfasting.

'Not if you say so, dear,' she replied absently.

'B . . . but . . .' began Gemma.

'There's that nervous stammer again,' said Shade, pouring orange juice for himself and Gemma. 'No buts! I'm taking you to see Niagara Falls.' His eyes eagerly scanned her features. 'Would you like that?'

'But . . .' Gemma began again, wondering if she would ever be allowed to finish a sentence. 'I thought Judge Dean was going to take me one day . . .'

'Toss you for it, Bradley,' said Shade.

'Oh, be my guest!' laughed Judge Dean. 'Clambering about the Falls is a young person's occupation.'

'Yes, Gemma, you go with Shade,' said Mrs Prescott. 'Bradley is taking me into Erie today. You'll have to hire a car, Shade, because we'll be using the Cadillac.'

'I'll see to it straight away,' said Shade, rising and going towards the telephone in the dining-room. 'Better get it for the week.'

It seemed pointless to argue further, so Gemma gave in resignedly. It was only a trip to the Falls, she told herself. So long as she kept it in mind that this man's feelings for her were capricious and slight she would be all right. Surely she could go out with him for the day without having to worry about being seduced! Surely she could endure his flippant inferences and casual caresses without getting hysterical! Heavens, it was the woman who called the tune, when all was said and done.

After breakfast she went to her room to change into a white gipsy blouse, poppy-red seersucker skirt and flat sandals. She was winding her hair into the usual knot at the nape of her neck when she heard the toot of a car horn outside.

She found Shade seated behind the wheel of a small open-topped sports car. He leaned across and opened the door for her then frowned as she took her seat.

'Must you always look like a schoolmarm?'

She gasped as he reached out both hands to attack her carefully coiled hair. She pulled away from him, but not before he had loosened the knot and shaken her hair about her shoulders, his touch sending tiny waves of alarm coursing through her.

'There, that's much better!' he said, starting up the engine and driving forward before she could take retaliatory action.

She glared at him. 'You've got a nerve!'

The wind snatched at her tresses and they streamed out behind her in a golden banner. She was aware of Shade's admiring glance. 'Keep your eyes on the road!' she ordered him.

They headed north through Buffalo and on to the State Thruway towards their destination, twenty-five miles away.

'I thought you were spending the vacation with Elgiva,' said Gemma, unable to hold her curiosity in check any longer.

'Whatever gave you that idea?' Shade asked innocently.

'Well, she seemed very keen not to accompany us here. I took it for granted that she was with you.'

'You shouldn't jump to conclusions,' Shade said quietly.

'She really likes you, you know.'

'Elgiva likes a lot of people.'

Gemma felt almost sorry for the girl. 'Is hers just another heart you're going to break? She's very young.'

'If Elgiva thinks she's in love with me, then I'm sorry, but I'm not attracted to her, I assure you. I haven't encouraged her either.'

'That's not true,' protested Gemma. 'I saw you two together at her homecoming party.'

He laughed suddenly. 'That was all a put-on, a gag. You couldn't have thought we were serious!'

'Well, I think she was!'

'Don't worry about Elgiva,' said Shade. 'She can take care of herself.'

Gemma had seen many photographs of Niagara, but nothing prepared her for the sheer majesty of the Horseshoe Falls. Standing midstream on Goat Island, they had a splendid view of the huge wall of rushing water that plunged down to send up clouds of spray.

'The water here is such a lovely green colour,' observed Gemma.

'That's pollution,' Shade disillusioned her. 'When Blondin crossed the falls on a tightrope over a hundred years ago the water was crystal clear.'

Far below in the gorge they could see a little boat sailing right into the spray. 'We'll do that trip this afternoon,' promised Shade. He saw Gemma blanch and grinned reassuringly. 'You'll be okay. I'll be right there with you, holding your hand.'

All America seemed to be picnicking in Prospect Park, and Gemma was amazed to see all the paraphernalia they had brought with them, from barbecue stoves to fine glassware. She was quite relieved when Shade bought their lunch from a hamburger-and-Coke stall. For all she had known he might have stowed a complicated lunch in the trunk of the car!

They found a sunny spot on the grass near some trees and spread the rug from the car.

'You look so much nicer with your hair loose,' said Shade, pulling the rings from the cans and handing her an ice-cold Coke. 'Promise you'll keep it like that for the rest of the holiday.'

She held her head to one side and trailed her fingers

through the golden curtain. 'If it pleases you, sir.'

As he bit into his hamburger, his eyes watched the movements of her hand until she felt every atom of her being glow beneath the burning intensity of his gaze.

Her senses surfaced like a diver coming up for air and she took a grip on her emotions. He was giving her the treatment and, forearmed with that knowledge, she could handle him!

He rose and walked to a litter bin to toss away the paper napkins and Coke tins, then, turning back towards her, began to unbutton his shirt, pulling it from the waistband of his shorts and revealing a mat of thick hair. Gemma dragged her eyes from his chest and experienced that same thrill in the pit of her stomach which she felt every time she was reminded of his devastating manliness.

She leaned her back against a tree and upturned her face to the sun. 'This is very pleasant.'

Shade arranged his body on the grass and rested his head on her lap. 'I hope you don't object to my doing this,' he looked up at her with a wicked smile on his mobile lips. 'But if you look around you, you'll see that the other couples are doing the same. We don't want to look odd.'

He closed his eyes and she had a strong urge to smooth back the lock of wavy hair which had fallen across his forehead—that dense black hair which had fascinated her at the interview in London. But she did not have the nerve, and she pulled restlessly at the daisies to keep her hands occupied.

They joined the queue for the boat *Maid of the Mist* and were issued with oilskins and hats. As they sailed into the cloud of spray, the boat rocked perilously and Gemma was glad of Shade's firm arm about her shoulders.

'There's a legend that once you're in the spray you can see the beautiful Indian maiden, Lelawale,' Shade shouted above the noise. 'She was sacrificed to the spirit of the harvest by being pushed over the edge of the falls. There she is! See her?'

Gemma stared. The spray could have represented anything, but she nodded vigorously.

Afterwards they explored the tunnels that ran behind the falls, once more donning the appropriate gear—rubber boots and black mackintoshes with hoods. They trudged the dark wet subterranean passages and Gemma jumped frequently as other misty figures loomed up in front of them from time to time. It was an eerie experience, but they had a splendid close-up view of the falls. The noise from the rushing cascades was deafening.

At one stage, Shade dragged Gemma towards a jet of water and pushed her face under it, then as she spluttered and gasped for breath he kissed her lips.

'It's supposed to be lucky!' he shouted as she felt the water get under the hood and begin to trickle down her back.

They were handed towels when they emerged from the tunnels, and Gemma darted an angry glance at Shade as she dried her shoulders beneath the elasticated top of her gipsy blouse.

He stole a sidelong glance at her furious face and said, 'What's a little water if you get lucky?'

As dusk fell they dined on a terrace overlooking the falls, which were spectacularly illuminated with coloured lights—four million candle-power, Shade informed Gemma knowledgeably.

She was pleasantly tired when they returned to the car and was content to sit quietly and let Shade do the talking. He told her about a recent horse sale he had attended and she found it only necessary to add the odd monosyllable.

Shade put the car in the garage and escorted her along the tree-lined path to the cottage. They were still in the shadows when he placed a hand on her shoulder and turned her round to face him.

She trembled as he buried his fingers in her tangled hair. 'It's so beautiful,' he whispered. 'Like spun gold. It fascinates me.'

'You don't say!' she laughed, pulling away from him.

The patio was in semi-darkness. As Gemma began to pick her way through the wrought-iron furniture, Shade barred her way. All at once his strong arms claimed her and his mouth pressed hard to hers, besieging her emotions and leaving her in a state of abject bewilderment. Her mind was a maelstrom of thoughts as the need for self-preservation fought with a wild flame of desire.

She felt his hands pulling gently at the top of her blouse and a cry of alarm escaped her lips. She dodged out of his embrace and pushed open the door to the deserted dining-room.

He darted after her. 'Gemma! Have a heart!'

'Thank you for a lovely day,' she said primly, her breath catching painfully in her throat as she strived for composure. 'Don't spoil it.'

'Spoil it? I want to enhance it.'

She stumbled towards the stairs. 'Is that why you took me out? In order to exact payment in kind?'

'You betcha sweet life!'

'Sorry, no way!'

The beam from the dimmed central light in the room fell on Shade's hair and cast his face with shadows through which shone the relentless steely glint from his eyes, boring into her with mesmeric fervour. Gemma's blood was racing through her veins and she would have been surprised to know how composed she appeared to him.

As they stared at each other the atmosphere became electric. It was as if someone had lit a quick-burning fuse and each waited for the explosion that was bound to come.

'You can't string me along for ever,' he muttered.

'You're stringing yourself along,' she snapped. 'I've made it quite clear . . .'

'Are you crazy? What man could resist the kind of challenge you've thrown out?'

His words brought a strange calmness to her. Her laugh was brittle. 'You're wasting your time!'

'It's my time!'

'Goodnight!' she said firmly.

'Don't be hard on yourself, Gemma,' he said, the old arrogance creeping back into his tone now that he could see she was adamant. 'I could be the answer to your maidenly frustration.'

Her eyes flashed indignantly. 'I don't think so!'

Shade thrust his hands into the pockets of his shorts and gave a philosophical shrug. 'So it's off to your virginal bed once more.' He sighed. 'And another cold shower for me!'

Gemma sped up the stairs to the safety of her room. She threw her bag on the dressing table, kicked off her sandals and lay full length on the bed, smiling up at the beamed ceiling. It really had been a most satisfactory day!

She was playing with fire, she knew. It had been almost too easy getting rid of Shade just now. He would not put up with much more of that treatment. Then what? The only answer appeared to be to refuse to accept any more of his invitations. But was she strong enough to say 'no', especially when Mrs Prescott seemed so keen to fall in with everything Shade suggested?

She rolled over to the edge of the bed and got to her feet, wondering again what had made him come to Buffalo so unexpectedly. Perhaps he and Elgiva had had words and he had departed in a huff to teach her a lesson. That would seem to be his style! Gemma wouldn't be surprised if Elgiva turned up here tomorrow. It was a daunting thought, but it would solve her own problems. It was difficult to know what to believe regarding Shade and Elgiva. He insisted there was nothing between them, but Elgiva told a different story! And Mrs Lambert had said the girl was a regular visitor to Five Oaks.

Gemma had to work hard on the accumulated letters the following morning, and it involved several phone calls to Mildred Yarwood, in solitary residence back at Clairmond. Mildred had forwarded all the correspondence on, but most of the information Gemma needed to answer it was in her little office.

The afternoon was spent accompanying Mrs Prescott to the beauty parlour in Buffalo to get the old lady 'prettied up', as she put it, for the ball to which they had all been invited that evening. It was to be held at the mansion next door to the cottage and was being given by the Gloriana Association—a kind of club for people who could trace their roots back to England.

In the early evening Gemma and Vikki sat together on the patio and sipped long cool drinks.

'Another one bites the dust!' grinned Vikki.

'What do you mean?'

'You've fallen for Shade like all the rest, my dear.'

Gemma regarded her friend and laughed easily. 'You're so wrong!'

'Come off it!' insisted Vikki. 'If I've ever seen a classic case of a woman in love, you're it!' She eyed Gemma obliquely. 'Careful, honey, that wolf hasn't got marriage on his mind. It could all end in tears.'

'I can take care of myself,' said Gemma.

Vikki rose as Shade came through the french windows. She gave him a long penetrating look before walking away into the garden.

'What's the matter with Vikki?' Shade moved one of the iron chairs nearer to Gemma. Turning it around, he sat astride it and leaned his arms on the back.

'That look was loaded!'

'She thinks you're the big bad wolf and I'm Little Red Riding Hood,' explained Gemma.

A smile lurked at the corner of his mouth and he allowed his eyes to travel lazily over her face and figure until she wriggled with embarrassment.

'My, what big eyes you have, Grandma?' she said facetiously.

'All the better to see you with!' He reached forward and grabbed a handful of hair at the back of her head, drawing her slowly but surely towards him. His kiss was smooth and lingering. He gave a low growl. 'I'll have the rest of the goodies in the basket after the ball tonight.'

Her mouth trembled. 'You will not . . .' she began.

He grinned smugly. 'You know I *will*, Gemma!'

Later Gemma brushed her hair until it shone, then put on a gown of rose-pink chiffon with long fringes crisscrossing the skirt, twenties-style.

The neckline was much too low, she thought, surveying herself in the long mirror. It had been Vikki's idea to buy this dress and Gemma had not been too keen at the time. Now she really had cold feet. It was too late to change and she cast around the room for something to preserve her modesty. Her eyes lit upon the vase of flowers on the windowsill, and she broke off a dark red carnation and placed it neatly into the top of the dress. That was better, she thought. She didn't want Shade ogling her all evening and coming to the conclusion that the basket of goodies was his for the taking!

Mrs Prescott looked regal in a beaded dress of black silk, while Shade and the Judge wore light-toned linen suits. Although the venue was nearby, Mrs Prescott had decided they would drive to the ball; she had put on a pair of high-heeled shoes and didn't want to risk a broken ankle getting there.

It was a small select affair and everyone was dressed

up to the hilt of fashion. An orchestra played middle-of-the-road music from past and present hit parades and Gemma was in great demand for the dancing. She enjoyed several with Shade and was impressed once more by the mastery of his dancing prowess.

They joined in a dance chain where the women went in one direction and the gentlemen in another. Each time the music stopped it was necessary to dance with the person immediately opposite in the chain. Several times Gemma just missed dancing with Shade, and she experienced a great sense of frustration as he grabbed hold of the woman next to her and spun away with his prize.

'You haven't danced with me yet, Shade,' said Mrs Prescott presently. 'I feel very put out about it.'

'Let's remedy that straight away,' said Shade, pulling the old lady to her feet and clasping her tightly for the tango.

Gemma sat down next to Bradley and idly watched the dancing couple. Shade was whispering into his partner's ear and the old lady was chuckling. Then he gripped her around the waist, bent her back in a very stylish dance movement, pulled her upright again and kissed her cheek.

Mrs Prescott was loving it! Shade certainly knew how to treat a woman. He had a separate approach for each of them. As Gemma watched she saw Shade and Mrs Prescott nearly jolted off their feet as an exuberant young couple backed into them. All four of them were profuse in their apologies, and Gemma observed the look of frank admiration on the face of the girl as she gazed at Shade. As the couples began to dance again, Shade caught the girl's eye over Mrs Prescott's shoulder and winked wickedly. Gemma experienced a little pang of resentment—and jealousy!

Oh, dear God, she thought, I'm in love with him!

The revelation hit her like a clenched fist—right in the stomach, winding her painfully. She gasped for breath as the idea took root.

'Are you okay, Gemma, my dear?' she heard Judge
Dean ask anxiously. 'You look kinda pale.'

She nodded and picked up her glass, rattling the ice
cubes. Dear, dear God! Vikki was right; she had fallen
for Shade like all the rest. Fallen for a tall good-looking
guy with square shoulders! From the start he had
intended using his undoubted magnetism to break down
her defences and bring her under his spell. And it had
worked!

Oh, she knew it wasn't a spiritual kind of love like
she had experienced with Rowan. That could never
happen again. But it was a kind of love nevertheless.
She wanted this man's arms around her, wanted to taste
his lips on hers. And more! Her thoughts sent the blood
pounding in her temples. Was that a kind of love? A
lustful love, perhaps. The kind that could only lead to
heartbreak. Her needs were for a permanent relationship—Shade's the exact opposite. According to him
a lustful love was the only kind . . .

She straightened as she saw the others coming back
to the table. She must get a hold of herself. She must
keep her knowledge secret. Giving in to her instincts
now would precipitate a catastrophe.

'Gee, that was good,' said Mrs Prescott, dropping
exhausted into her chair. 'Shade, you are a charmer!'

He bent low over her hand. 'I know what my women
want,' he murmured intimately.

Gemma jumped. He could have been reading her
mind.

Mrs Prescott had sagged in her chair. 'I'm tired,' she
moaned.

Gemma stood up eagerly. 'I'll take you home.'
Anything to get away from Shade, to get out of having
to go home with him. She needed time to think over
this new turn of events.

'No, you stay and enjoy yourself,' said her employer.

'Bradley will take me home. You two can walk.'

The ball would not start breaking up until the early hours and Gemma wondered how she was going to survive until then—knowing what she knew. Uppermost in her mind was the thought that she must keep her head and not let Shade suspect the way she felt about him.

They played the last waltz at one o'clock and Gemma could hardly think straight, held in Shade's arms, barely moving, with the lights dimmed.

The number of guests was sadly depleted now, for most of the older people had retired early. The remaining dancers joined hands for 'Auld Lang Syne' and wished their hosts goodnight.

Shade picked up Gemma's stole and placed it about her shoulders. 'Think you can make it home in those shoes?' He eyed her stiletto heels. 'Or shall I get a cab? Better still, I could carry you.'

'It's only a few yards,' she replied. 'I'll be okay.'

Outside, Shade wrapped an arm around her, holding her so tightly that she had no option but to place her arm about his waist. We must look like lovers, she thought crazily.

The night sky was like black velvet sprinkled with diamonds, and like velvet it had the effect of smothering all noise except for the faint murmuring of the lake. Not a bird stirred, not a breath of air stole through the pines. Gemma's nostrils caught the drugging perfume of jasmine and roses and other scents she could not distinguish.

'You're very quiet, honey,' observed Shade.

'I'm tired,' she lied. Her senses had never been more alert to the sights, sounds and smells all around her. The lodge was in darkness and they crept past in order not to wake the Judds, tiptoeing over the flagstones until they reached the cottage.

One low-wattage lantern burned in the hall. Shade

closed the door silently. He watched her, a sensual smile deepening about his mouth, then with a quick movement of his hand he flicked the carnation from her cleavage. 'You don't need that!' he remarked, feasting his eyes on her heavy bosom.

Gemma offered no resistance as his hands caught her shoulders and she felt the crushing pressure of his mouth, forcing her lips apart till her head spun dizzily. His fingers slid through her hair, holding her head still while his mouth explored hers again, a gentle kiss this time, sweet and lingering.

She swayed on her feet and clung to him for support as her mind was thrown into chaos. She was frightened by the depths of her feelings. She had to stop this now—for her sake; for his sake. Because it wasn't fair!

'Stop!' she laughed nervously when he withdrew his lips. 'You take my breath away. You must have had a lot of practice to kiss like that!'

'I told you, I'm a Harvard man. It comes natural.'

Reality finally penetrated her brain. Somehow she had to get up the stairs and into her room—alone.

CHAPTER EIGHT

'I'M tired,' she said, feigning a yawn. 'Goodnight, Shade.'

She walked quickly towards the stairs, her heart in her mouth, half expecting him to chase after her. But glancing briefly over her shoulder she observed him still standing by the door, leaning against the jamb, his arms folded.

She couldn't believe her good fortune and sped up the stairs. However, by the time she had reached her door he had caught up with her. He seized a thick hank of her hair and, none too gently, jerked her head backwards.

She gave a little cry of pain. 'Leave me alone!' she snapped, glancing anxiously along the corridor.

'You're not sending me away again,' he said. 'Even you wouldn't be so cruel.'

Gemma gathered her wits about her and disentangled her hair from his fingers. 'I want you to go!' she said.

'Liar!'

They faced each other obstinately, both breathing deeply. Oh lord, she thought, if only I could get through that door!

'Gemma!' His voice was sharpened with impatience. 'I want to make love to you!'

'I know very well what you want,' she retorted in a loud whisper. 'You don't have to spell it out. There's no need to broadcast it all over the house.' She grasped the door handle as her self-control came near to running out. 'But I'm afraid you're still wasting your time.'

Surprisingly he stood back from her and made a mocking bow. 'Don't count on it!' he replied smoothly as she slipped through the aperture and closed the door on him.

Gemma was trembling all over as she went to the long mirror. She stared at her reflection, seeing herself as he had seen her, the glow on her cheeks, her lips parted, her hair a delightful tangle, the dress's décolletage revealing the firmly rounded contours of her breasts.

A great feeling of despondency came over her. What was the matter with her? She had done the right thing sending him away. No good could come from letting herself be carried away by him. Then why was she shaking? Why did she feel she had missed out on something wonderful?

In the streaks of moonlight filtering through the slats of the venetian blinds, the colours of the flowering plants on the window sill—magnolias, orange blossoms and camellias—came out brilliantly and the air was heavy with the fragrance, stifling her with its poignancy. Gemma manoeuvred the cord to raise the blinds and her breath caught in her throat at the scene of stirring beauty outside, the lake shimmering in the moonlight, the sky soft and impenetrable. It was as if the whole of nature conspired to call her a fool.

She allowed the blinds to fall again and a terrible ache filled her body. Listlessly she took off her dress and hung it in the wardrobe, then went into her bathroom to remove every trace of make-up.

It was then that some kind of force outside her control took over, which made her search through her cupboards for the white nightdress which had caught her eye when she had gone shopping with Vikki. Their conversation, as she had dithered over it, came into her mind. 'Who will see it?' she had asked, and Vikki had replied mischievously, 'You never know!'

The pure silk clung sensuously to her body and the deep lace of the hem billowed about her ankles in luxurious folds. She fastened the tiny pearl button on the bodice and adjusted the dainty narrow straps.

Suddenly she pulled a face at her reflection. What kind of madness was making her behave in this way, as if she expected Shade to come through that door at any moment? It was ridiculous. And yet the words 'Don't count on it!' kept sounding in her ears.

She remembered something else Vikki had said. 'Men like him revel in the conquest but are not interested in the responsibility.'

Gemma doused the lights except for the small lamp shining above the dressing table and sat down on the plush stool to brush her hair. Gradually, as she sorted out the tangles, she also sorted out her confused mind. She had no intention of being another scalp for Shade Lambert's belt, and the sooner he got that into his head the better. Correction—the sooner she got it into her own head! Okay, so she had fallen under the spell of his undoubted charm! So what? It didn't mean she had to go to pieces and throw away every vestige of moral fibre she possessed.

She felt more at ease now and picked up a jar of night cream, intending to slap it all over her face and thus convince herself once and for all that she was going to spend the night alone.

She had unscrewed the lid when she saw, in the mirror reflection, the door open and Shade slip quietly into the room. She rose to her feet in consternation and pressed herself into the deep recess of the dormer window. It was all very well dreaming, but the reality was a different matter.

He had changed into an olive-green bathrobe which swung open to reveal a pair of black jeans. His hair was damp and he brought into the room a tangy smell of fresh cologne.

He grinned lopsidedly at her. 'Those cold showers aren't effective any more.'

He covered the distance between them in long strides, then stopped dead, his eyes taking in her natural beauty, her face devoid of make-up, her shining hair, the way the material of the nightdress left little to the imagination.

Gemma still held the jar of night cream and lifted it menacingly. 'What . . . what are you doing here?' she demanded.

Shade calmly took the jar from her hand and set it down on the dressing table. Then he took her wrist in an unbreakable grip to jerk her from the recess and into his arms.

His kiss was devastating, draining her of all her will to resist him. His lips ravaged hers, forcing her to respond and sending shivers of ecstasy coursing the length of her spine.

She pushed weakly against his chest in an attempt to be free of him, to give her time to think, but only succeeded in causing her pulses to quicken as her fingers made contact with the thick black jungle of hair and the rippling muscles. His flesh was slightly damp and his heart was thumping in unison with her own.

His lips fastened on hers again, hard and intense, while his fingers raked her hair, pulling at the roots.

Suddenly, in complete contrast, he lifted his head to place a tender kiss on her temple, caressing her throat with his fingers and unnerving her to a state of hysteria.

'You want me to make love to you,' he whispered, his mouth burning a trail from her temple to her lips. 'It's what you want, isn't it?'

She denied it with a vigorous shake of her head, for her throat was dry and incapable of speech.

'No?' His eyes surveyed her intently.

'No!' she moaned.

His mouth silenced her and she felt herself being swept along on a tidal wave of passion. Even as she struggled against him a bolt of pleasure charged her body. It was like being up against an irresistible force, a sensual power that it would be useless to fight. She felt his fingers dig into her shoulders and took pleasure from the pain. The breath quavered perfidiously in her throat and she was beyond all rationalising. 'Please,' she begged, 'You mustn't . . .'

Shade carefully undid the pearl button on the front of her nightdress, then slipped the narrow shoulder straps down until her full breasts fell into his hands.

He gave a little grunt and swung her into his arms to place her gently, almost reverently on the bed, his eyes devouring her silky flesh and the mass of thick hair which had spread itself in a golden cloud on the pillow, one luxuriant strand veiling her flushed cheek.

A moment later she became trapped under the avalanche of his body weight. As he lowered his mouth to tease a coral-pink nipple she was aware of a deep ache within her. There was no longer any need to keep her secret from him. 'Shade,' she whispered, pushing her fingers into his hair, 'I love you.'

He held himself still and she felt his body slacken. Slowly his hands fastened over hers and pulled them away from his hair as he stared at her, a dark brooding look on his face.

'What's the matter?' she asked fearfully.

A muscle jerked in his jaw and his eyes narrowed to a black intensity. For long moments he seemed to be wrestling with his thoughts, his brows drawn together, then all at once he pushed her away from him and stood up.

'Shade!' she cried as he walked towards the door. 'Come back!' She struggled to a sitting position and hastily covered her nakedness.

The sharp metallic click of the closing door snapped her out of her daze. It was as if a bucket of cold water had been thrown in her face.

Moments later she heard a distant door slam and

someone walking along the gravel path outside the house.

She fought for composure, but the tears won. She viewed the room as through a heavy mist, then rolled over to bury her face in the pillows. Her mind was a turmoil of agonising doubts. She had been brought to the brink of ecstasy—then rejected. The fire still burned in the core of her body, a searing pain that consumed every fibre of her nerves. She had been eager to surrender despite her moral upbringing, despite the knowledge that nothing good could come from this wild passion except appeasement of her carnal need—and she had been cast aside. The promise had not been fulfilled. She felt exposed and vulnerable.

Her tears had saturated the pillowcase and her hair stuck to her face in moist streaks. How could one person weep so much and live? she wondered.

After a while her crying subsided into a whimper and she fell into a troubled sleep.

The following morning she was late getting down to breakfast. Her eyes were puffy and red-rimmed from so much crying and she had no wish to be questioned. More important, she had no wish to see Shade Lambert's face across the table.

She donned a high-necked, long-sleeved dress as if to mask herself from prying eyes, and put on a pair of sunglasses. She even left her hair loose so that she could hide behind it.

As she reached the top of the stairs she was irked to see Shade below her, sitting on the bottom stair, his ear to the hall telephone. She studied his broad back. He wore a chequered lumberjack shirt and was smoking a rare cigarette.

Gemma kept still, choosing to wait for him to finish his call rather than push by him.

'Calm down, Elgiva,' he was saying. 'How can I make head or tail of it if you insist on crying?'

Gemma drew back, not wanting to eavesdrop, but his voice floated clearly up to her. 'Listen, honey, it'll be okay. If marriage is what you want then so be it! Trust me!'

Marriage? He was discussing marriage with Elgiva!

Gemma decided she could listen no longer and she clattered noisily down the stairs.

Shade glanced over his shoulder, then stood up to allow her to pass. 'Goodbye, sweetheart,' he said into the phone. 'And don't worry.'

Gemma swept into the deserted dining-room and out on to the patio, her thoughts tumbling over each other in rapid succession. She understood everything now. Shade was in love with Elgiva. Why else had he acted so strangely the night before? He had delighted in stringing Gemma along to satisfy his male pride, eliciting a declaration of love from her as just another conquest. He had placed her heart under siege from the word 'go'. Then, at the crucial moment, when he could have accepted Gemma's unconditional surrender, he had been haunted by his love for Elgiva. Gemma grudgingly admitted that it was to his credit that he had elected to stay faithful to the girl he loved. Now Elgiva was in some kind of trouble and he was concerned only for her.

Gemma's reasoning acted like a cold March wind on her emotions. She had been duped.

After three cups of coffee she went in search of Mrs Prescott, warily turning each corner in the rambling house, in case she ran into Shade again. But her employer told her that the two men had gone out in the boat to do some fishing.

It was late evening before they returned. Gemma was in the kitchen talking to the cook when Judge Dean entered the back door, proudly holding up a skewer from which hung a dozen or so plump trout.

'I caught these,' he announced gleefully. 'Shade was

decidedly off form today.'

Good, thought Gemma maliciously, hoping his conscience, for the way he had treated her, was the cause of his bad day. No, more likely his concern for Elgiva, she thought dejectedly.

'He's gone into Buffalo now,' the Judge went on. 'Said he had to see a man about a horse. He won't be back for dinner.' He eyed Gemma contemplatively. 'Have you two had a row?'

Gemma passed a weary hand across her brow. 'I don't want to talk about it.'

She was quiet through dinner and decided on an early night.

'Yes, you look rather haggard,' smiled Mrs Prescott.

Gemma doubted she would be able to sleep and remembered having seen a Jack Higgins thriller in the library, just the kind of thing she needed to take her mind off her present problems. She entered the little room and was surprised to see Shade standing by the window, a cup and saucer in his hand.

They stared at each other, then he pushed the fingers of his free hand through his hair in a vaguely nervous gesture. Taking courage from that small sign, she said scathingly, 'You may well hide from me!'

He gave a start, stung by her words. For a moment a look of contrition crossed his features and he appeared to be about to say something to vindicate himself for his callous behaviour the previous night. Then his face hardened and it was as if a steel shutter came down over his eyes. 'Have you come for some more of the same treatment?' he asked sardonically.

Gemma recoiled from the harshness of his words and her spirit plummeted like a dead bird. 'I . . . I came for a book,' she stammered.

'That's what you say!' He placed the cup and saucer on the windowsill and stepped towards her. 'Don't you know when you've had enough?'

She backed away from him, frightened by his menacing tone and the intensity of his stare. 'Please . . .'

He seized her arms in a grip of iron and dragged her towards him, holding her against the hardness of his body.

'Let me go!' She felt the tears stinging her eyes.

His mouth assaulted hers, contemptuously forcing her lips apart, while his hands moved ruthlessly over her body, every action guaranteed to punish.

Shade released her and she touched her bruised lips. 'You monster!' she cried. 'What have I done to deserve that?'

Again a softness entered his eyes, but it was fleeting and the armour plating fell sharply into place once more. 'Go away, little girl!' He calmly picked up the cup and saucer. 'You're out of your league!'

Her temper boiled over and she struck out at him, hitting his face with the flat of her hand and knocking his head sideways. The handle of the cup broke off with a loud snap and the delicate china shattered on the floor, its contents soaking into the carpet.

'Guess I had that coming,' he observed mildly, with a slight shrug.

His quiet rejoinder was totally unexpected and for a moment she stared at his darkening cheek, her palm still smarting from the impact.

'You despicable man!' she spat at him. 'How dare you kiss me in that loathsome way! You have no decent feelings whatsoever!'

She fled from the room and paused outside the door. She was shaking to the depths of her being and felt slightly cheated that Shade had offered no word in his defence.

Hot tears scalded her cheeks. 'Love hurts' he had said. Her relationship with Rowan had been naïve, childish almost. She had spoken so glibly of the real thing and she had known nothing. Shade Lambert had changed all that. She had never experienced such pain, such humiliation. He had torn her tender emotions out by the roots for the simple satisfaction of throwing them back in her face.

She knew all about the real thing now.

The following morning Gemma and Mrs Prescott walked along beside the lake to the little Anglican church for the Whit Sunday service. The sight of the flowers and greenstuffs around the pulpit made Gemma homesick for her Buckinghamshire village. For the first time since she had come to America she longed for the comfort of things familiar. 'There'll be times when things go wrong', her mother had said. 'It's nice then to have your family to cushion your fall'. How she needed them now!

When they returned to the cottage Vikki informed them that Shade had left suddenly to return to Kentucky.

Gemma could not prevent the little gasp that escaped her and she squirmed under her employer's curious glance.

'I expect he's missing Elgiva,' said Mrs Prescott.

Gemma went straight to her room to change. There was no time to surrender to the utter despondency which threatened to tear her apart. They were entertaining several guests for lunch and she had to get into a jolly mood, a mood in which she must laugh and pretend to be enjoying herself, to be the perfect companion.

The next four days dragged by with endless bridge games and uneventful mornings on the boat. Before Shade had arrived Gemma had been enjoying the bridge and the sailing, she reflected. He had spoilt everything.

She played so badly at cards that Mrs Prescott was prompted to ask if she were sickening for something.

'You do look pale, dear,' she said solicitously. 'I hope I'm not overworking you.'

'You overwork me all you like,' said Gemma grimly. 'The more work you can give me the better I shall like it.'

The vacation finally came to an end and Gemma supervised the packing of Mrs Prescott's trunks. The Judge had been elected to drive the Cadillac back to Kentucky and he suggested Gemma accompany him to share the driving and help alleviate the monotony.

Gemma jumped at the idea. The Judge was good company; she would be able to relax away from Mrs Prescott's beck and call; and driving the Cadillac would give her something positive to think about.

'Yes, you go with Bradley,' said Mrs Prescott when Gemma presented the idea to her. 'It might do you good.' She turned to the judge. 'Look after her, Bradley. Good companions are hard to come by. I shall be eternally grateful to Shade for finding you, Gemma.'

Gemma acknowledged the compliment ruefully. It would have been better if she'd never answered that advertisement.

They set out very early to travel the four hundred miles south to Lexington, and the Judge took the first stint at the wheel. He sensed her preoccupation with her own troubles and kept up a lively conversation, telling her about the famous landmarks of the towns through which they passed—the first Mormon Temple at Cleveland Heights and the State Reformatory at Mansfield.

They reached Columbus by noon and the Judge swung the car into the parking lot of a riverside hotel. Lunch was being served on a long picturesque terrace and they were shown to a secluded booth with a wealth of climbing plants separating them from their fellow diners. Below them was an immaculate lawn where blue-flowering jacaranda trees gave welcome shade to strutting white peacocks and the surface of a pool broke to show the gleam of a gold fin.

'Right,' said the Judge, after they had ordered. 'What's all this about?'

She looked up to see him studying her, his eyes sympathetic.

'I don't know what you mean,' she answered haughtily.

'Look at it this way.' His tone held a dry brittle note. 'Everything is fine and dandy, then suddenly Shade arrives. A couple of days later you start crying and Shade flies out in a hurry.'

Her jaw tightened. It was no use denying it. The Judge had seen her red eyes and he wasn't a fool.

His eyes continued to probe her expression intently. 'I'm a good listener.'

She laid down her fork and her shoulders slumped despondently. 'Oh, Judge!' She blinked rapidly to keep the tears at bay. 'I'm all mixed up.'

'Came on strong, did he?'

Her smile broke through at his choice of words. How American! 'He sure did!' she drawled.

'Then dropped you like a hot potato?' He smiled gently. 'Cheer up! You're not the first and you won't be the last.'

'That's no consolation at all.'

'I know.' His hand covered hers in a fatherly way. 'But weep no more, my lady. Things can only improve now.' He pointed to her untouched shrimp cocktail. 'I hope you're not going to starve yourself on account of him. He's not worth it, you know.' He reached across the table to lift a forkful of food to her lips.

Gemma took it, like a baby, and he placed the fork in her hand. 'What happens now?' he asked.

'Forget him, I suppose.'

It was Gemma's turn to drive and she found it exhilarating handling the gears of the large handsome car. She had enough to do thinking about driving on the right and observing all the unfamiliar road signs without concerning herself with any emotional troubles she had.

Judge Dean leaned back against the head-rest and said angrily, 'If I were a young man, I'd thrash Shade Lambert!'

'There's no need to on my account,' said Gemma, without thinking. 'Nothing happened at Buffalo.'

The Judge was silent for a moment digesting this piece of information, then he let out a low whistle. 'I see. You're not mad at him for what he did, but for what he didn't do! I was forgetting the intricacies of a woman's mind.'

Gemma's vision was blurred with sudden tears. She knew she was driving too fast; Yarwood had warned her that the conception of speed was deceptive when driving such a smooth silent-running car.

'Hey, you're travelling a bit!' exclaimed the Judge. 'Slow down or you'll miss the lights at the next intersection.'

She slammed on the brakes, but it was too late. The traffic lights changed to red and the car overshot the white line. A moment later there came a loud crunch as a small red Chrysler truck ran into them. Fortunately they had almost come to a halt and the other vehicle had just started up, so the impact was slight.

'Are you okay?' asked Judge Dean, peering into Gemma's white face.

She nodded numbly and got shakily out of the car. There was a big dent in the front door of the Cadillac and a streak of red paint from the truck's wing.

Other cars began honking their horns and all at once a police car pulled up beside them. A gum-chewing traffic cop, wearing a large pair of sunglasses, got out and walked slowly towards them.

During the next half an hour, the Judge proved to be a tower of strength. He produced Gemma's international driving licence and insurance papers and exchanged names and addresses with the other driver. He explained

that Gemma was a visitor to the country and unfamiliar
with the car. The policeman seemed to accept this explanation and told her he had a sister living in 'Wor-
ces-ter-shire'. After some deliberation he said he would
let her off with a caution. Gemma agreed to accept responsibility for the accident and make good the damage
to the other vehicle. They shook hands all round.

'I don't know what Henrietta is going to say, I'm
sure,' murmured Judge Dean as he pushed Gemma into
the passenger's seat and took the wheel himself. 'Still,
the damage is comparatively slight and we can drive the
car home.'

Gemma burst into tears. Crashing the Cadillac
seemed to be the last straw.

'Don't take on so,' said the Judge kindly. 'I'll tell her
it was my fault if you like.' He grinned. 'It was in a
way.'

'That won't be necessary,' she sobbed. 'I'll face the
music.'

Mrs Prescott was extremely vexed when she saw the
damage to the car, but she forgave Gemma magnanim-
ously. Yarwood was a different matter. You'd think he
owned the car! thought Gemma. He ranted and raved
and uttered threats until she thought he would burst a
blood vessel.

'I have to go down to the local television studio this
evening,' said Mrs Prescott over an early dinner. 'A
message was waiting for me when I arrived home.
Something's come up about a conservation area we're
trying to save and the television company want my views
on the subject on a live show.' She glanced at Gemma's
pale complexion, the dark patches beneath her eyes. 'I
don't think you'd better come with me. I'll take
Bradley.'

'Oh, I'll be all right,' protested Gemma. 'I don't want
to let you down.'

'No, you have an early night,' insisted Mrs Prescott.

'I don't like the look of you at all. Perhaps you've caught a chill. Will you be all right left on your own?'

'Of course,' said Gemma. 'Why? Isn't Elgiva here?'

'She was here when we returned this afternoon,' said Mrs Prescott, 'but she's gone out again and said she might not be back tonight. Goodness knows what she's up to. Anyway, Mildred will be in, in the apartment over the garage, if you should want anything. You can get her on the house phone.'

'I'll be all right,' insisted Gemma.

The house was quiet after the others had left and it was something of a relief to be able to relax. Gemma went to her own apartment, but knew she would not be able to sleep so read the latest edition of *Harper's Bazaar* until it was time to turn on the television set to catch Mrs Prescott's interview.

It was ten o'clock before the programme went out and Gemma hoped the old lady was not overdoing things so soon after her flight home from Buffalo. However, she seemed very alert and put her views over clearly and succinctly. She could certainly teach the young people a thing or two about sticking to the point, thought Gemma admiringly.

She got up and switched off the set, then went into her bathroom to take a quick shower. She had put on a terry bathrobe and was making herself a cup of tea in the curtained recess when a sound came to her ears from outside in the corridor, like someone knocking against one of the little tables which cluttered the place.

Mrs Prescott could not have returned already, she reasoned, because the 'live' programme had only ended ten minutes ago.

Gemma quietly opened the door and stepped out into the corridor, just in time to see Todd Ives leaning over and straightening a lacquered table. At the sight of her he drew himself to his full height. 'Hi!'

'Todd Ives! What are you doing here?' she gasped,

her eyes straying to the door of the room housing the silver collection. It was closed.

'Why, I came to see you, honey,' he grinned, allowing his indolent gaze to travel over her untidily-piled hair and the robe clinging to her damp body.

She had only ever seen him in soiled working clothes and was surprised to see how smart he looked in a dark suit with his red hair neatly combed. He was quite handsome, she realised with a start, and younger than she had first supposed—in his mid-twenties.

'Don't be funny!' she snapped. 'What are you doing here?'

'Just visiting.' His eyes gleamed with unconcealed excitement, almost verging on the ecstatic. What was he up to?

Gemma bit her lip in consternation. 'How did you get in?'

'I rang the bell and no one answered . . .'

She wanted to call him a liar. 'I've been here all evening . . .' Then she remembered, she had been listening to the television and taken a shower, both noisy activities. 'How did you get in?' she asked again.

'I tried the front door, but it was locked, so I went round to the back door which wasn't.'

'So you just walked in?'

'Yep!' He fingered his shaggy moustache. 'I shouted out a couple of times, but no one answered.'

'So you came upstairs? You had no right . . .'

He shrugged. 'Okay, I'll go.'

'Perhaps you should wait till Mrs Prescott comes home and see what she thinks,' said Gemma.

'I must go!' he said, turning on the heel of an elegant boot. 'One of the horses . . .'

'Oh yes,' she sneered, 'one of the horses.' A thought occurred to her. 'Perhaps I'd better ring Shade . . .'

'I shouldn't do that, honey!' Todd tossed over his shoulder, 'He's been like a bear with a sore head since he returned from Buffalo.'

Gemma watched the tall retreating figure and called out, 'I shall have to report this to Mrs Prescott.'

'Whatever you think best, honey,' said Todd, then with a laugh he ran down the stairs and she heard the front door slam.

Gemma went straight to the door of the room housing the silver collection. It was locked. Then she sped down the stairs to the back door to see if Todd could, in fact, have come in that way. That too was locked, but she saw that the window was on the catch. She did not know what to do—call the police, or wait to see what Mrs Prescott said. The old lady would be very angry to think that Todd had been prowling around. Then there was Gemma's promise to Shade not to cause any trouble for Todd.

Shade! Everything always came back to him, she thought irritably.

She went to the telephone in the drawing-room and lifted the receiver, working herself up to dial his number. She wanted desperately to hear his deep resonant voice. At the same time she wanted nothing more to do with him. She took a deep breath and dialled the Five Oaks number. She spoke to one of his staff and was trembling violently by the time he came on the line.

'Gemma?' he asked huskily. 'What's the matter . . .?'

She cut into his words with relish. 'This is not a social call. I've just caught Todd Ives prowling around upstairs at Clairmond.'

He caught his breath sharply. 'The devil you have!'

'I'll have to tell Mrs Prescott about it.'

'Calm down!' There was a curt inflection in his voice. 'There's no need to make things more difficult for Todd than they already are.'

'Not make things more difficult . . .? He was trespassing, despite being told to keep away. Personally, I think he's paranoiac.'

'If he's done any damage I'll cover the bill,' said Shade

urgently. 'But I doubt if he has. Please don't tell Mrs Prescott. I'll talk to him and see he never does it again. I'll stand guarantee for him . . .'

Gemma took great pleasure in banging the receiver down hard. A few minutes later Mrs Prescott and Judge Dean came in the door.

'Gemma!' said Mrs Prescott crossly. 'Why aren't you in bed?'

The Judge detected the anger burning in Gemma's eyes. 'What's up?'

Gemma made up her mind quickly. 'Todd Ives was here.'

'Here?' echoed Mrs Prescott, looking ready to faint and leaning heavily on the Judge's arm for support.

'He was upstairs in the corridor.'

Mrs Prescott sank slowly on to the settee. 'The silver! Oh, Bradley . . .'

'It's all right,' said Gemma quickly. 'I'm sure he didn't touch anything in there. The door is still locked.'

'I don't understand,' mused Bradley. 'How did he get in?'

'The window in the kitchen was open,' said Gemma. 'I didn't notice it before I went upstairs.'

'That's right,' said Mrs Prescott. 'I remember asking Mildred to open it to let out the smell of that burnt pan.'

'Do you want me to call the police, Henrietta?' asked the Judge.

Mrs Prescott considered the idea. 'No,' she said slowly. 'I'll handle Todd Ives. If he ever comes here again, I'll be ready for him. I have a revolver in my bedroom drawer.'

Gemma's head was reeling. She felt almost sorry for Todd and couldn't believe he was a thief despite having found him in such suspicious circumstances.

Elgiva put in an appearance at lunch the following day

and offered no explanation for her absence from the house the previous night. Gemma wondered if she had been with Shade. Perhaps she had been there when he had answered the phone.

'Well, we had some excitement last night,' grumbled Mrs Prescott. 'We had Todd Ives here sneaking about upstairs.'

'Oh, I wish I'd been here,' giggled Elgiva. 'I'd love to have seen you send him packing, Gran.'

'I didn't send him packing,' growled Mrs Prescott. 'If I had he'd have needed hospitalisation. No, Gemma caught him.'

'How intriguing!' Elgiva smiled across at Gemma. 'Say, you look nice with your hair loose. Not so cold and aloof.'

Gemma acknowledged the backhanded compliment with a slight nod. She didn't know why she continued to wear her hair in the style Shade preferred. Yes, she did! It was in the hope that he would call round. What a fool she was!

Elgiva carefully folded her table napkin into a small square. 'Shade is sending Todd over to pick me up this afternoon, Gran. You won't shoot him, will you?'

'What's that?' demanded Mrs Prescott. 'If that man sets foot on my property, I'll blast him to Kingdom come!'

Elgiva sighed. 'In that case I'll have to ring Shade and ask him to come himself.'

'What are you up to, Elgiva?' asked Mrs Prescott.

'Shade and I are going away for a couple of days' vacation. To . . . to sort things out.'

'But he's just been away!' spluttered Mrs Prescott. 'And you're due back at secretarial college, aren't you?'

Gemma felt a strange numbness chilling her heart.

'This is more important than college,' said Elgiva. 'It's very special and affects my whole life.' She rose before Mrs Prescott could say anything further. 'I must go and get changed.'

'Young hussy!' snorted Mrs Prescott. 'Eighteen years old and going away with Shade!' She lifted her head and gazed thoughtfully at the ceiling. 'Still, he would be some catch. The Prescotts and the Lamberts connected by marriage. I like the idea.'

Gemma leaned back in her chair. 'Going away for a couple of days isn't the same as getting married.'

'No, but it could lead to it,' said the old lady. 'It would be a relief to see her settled with a good man.' She warmed to the theme. 'I love weddings! We could hold it here—get Pierremont to cater and Saint-Lucien to do the flowers.' She paused. 'Why, Gemma, what's the matter, dear?'

'Will you excuse me?' said Gemma, getting up from her chair and heading for the door. 'I've got a splitting headache.'

As she left the room she heard Mrs Prescott remark to the maid, 'Poor Gemma, I think she's still suffering from the effects of the crash.'

Gemma, lingering in one of the upstairs rooms, watched out for Shade's arrival all afternoon. Futile as it seemed, she had a desperate longing to see his face, if only for an instant. She ached for a glimpse of him—so arrogant, so coolly mocking, but the only man she could ever love.

His Porsche arrived at last and she kept out of sight behind the lace drapes.

She watched him bound up the steps and heard the doorbell ring distantly in the house. Moments later Elgiva came out. Shade took the girl's overnight bag and they both got into the car. So they really were going away together!

A tear rolled down Gemma's cheeks. She loved him. She hated him.

When Elgiva returned two days later she was bubbling with excitement.

Gemma was cataloguing books in the library under Mrs Prescott's guidance when the young girl rushed in shouting, 'I'm back, Gran!'

'Nice trip?' enquired Mrs Prescott drily.

Elgiva sat on the arm of her grandmother's chair. 'Fabulous!' She took off her chic red beret and sent it skimming across the room.

Gemma, perched on a stepladder, concentrated on her work. The room was filled with the rich smell of the leather-tooled, gold-lettered books, and the unstained sycamore shelves glinted like satin in the sunlight streaming through the tall windows.

'Oh, Gran,' enthused Elgiva, 'I'm in love. You can't know how it feels . . .'

'I think I can,' sniffed Mrs Prescott. 'I may be in my dotage, as far as you're concerned, but I have had a moment or two.'

'You darling!' Elgiva bent to kiss the withered cheek, then straightened to take off her black linen coat, revealing a red tube dress underneath.

'Holy Moses! You look like a tart!' observed Mrs Prescott.

'It's only the latest fashion,' protested Elgiva.

Gemma thought the girl looked positively lovely, so smart and sophisticated. Her bare shoulders gleamed like ivory. Had Shade's lips kissed them before she left him? Had his fingers slid through that long brown hair?

'Do you know what's the most wonderful experience in the world?' asked Elgiva, walking to the window and staring out over the lawns.

'No, but I have a feeling you're going to tell me,' said Mrs Prescott.

Elgiva turned, her face radiant. 'It's when the man you love loves you.'

Gemma climbed down from the stepladder. 'Shall we call it a day?' she asked, glancing at her watch.

Elgiva looked quickly at Gemma and a brief expression of pity and understanding crossed her face. She looked as if she were about to commiserate and Gemma felt she couldn't stand that. Then Elgiva smiled gently and said, 'Cheer up, Gemma, your turn will come.'

Gemma crept upstairs to her apartment and sat listlessly on the bed. She might as well forget Shade now.

She counted on her fingers the few dates she had had with him, the twenty or so times they had met. So few occasions—and yet they had changed her whole existence. She had built a dream on a few kisses. No, it went back farther than that. She had loved him right from the start, since that cold day in London when they had struck sparks off each other. Why else had she agreed to accept the job? Well, it was all past history now.

As she got things into perspective, it was like closing a chapter on her life. Except that there was no new chapter to turn to. She had reached the end of the book.

CHAPTER NINE

A COUPLE of days later, Mrs Prescott and Vikki journeyed into Lexington to choose some new curtain material for the back of the house, leaving Gemma to hunt for some old insurance policies which appeared to have been mislaid.

She was in the drawing-room sorting through the desk when she heard someone cross the hall singing, 'Here comes the bride!' It was a female voice, getting nearer, and Gemma surmised it was Mildred coming to collect the coffee tray. She was surprised, therefore, to see Elgiva enter the room and cross to the tall window overlooking the front steps.

At the sight of Gemma, the girl emitted a loud gasp and faltered, 'I ... I thought you'd gone out with the others.'

Gemma rose from her chair and stared open-mouthed at the young girl. Elgiva was arrayed in a short white lace dress and on her head nestled a white satin pillbox hat with a jaunty curled feather and tiny spotted veil. A wedding outfit! thought Gemma.

Elgiva actually blushed. 'Don't look so surprised. You knew it was on the cards.'

'Are you eloping?' asked Gemma in an awed whisper.

'It looks that way.' Elgiva continued to the window and peered out anxiously. 'Shade's sending Todd round to pick me up any moment now. I thought I'd planned it pretty good, but I didn't count on finding you still here.'

'But why do you have to elope?' gasped Gemma. 'What will your grandmother say?'

'Oh, she'll be furious with me. But she'll have to get over it.'

Gemma took a step towards the girl. 'Must you behave like this?' she asked earnestly. 'Why not wait and talk things over? Mrs Prescott has no objections to your marrying Shade.'

'No!' cried Elgiva. 'It's got to be this way. Everything's arranged.' She turned and grabbed Gemma's hands. 'You won't tell her, will you? She'll only try to stop me.'

'I must tell her.'

'Yes, I guess you must.' Elgiva's expression clouded over. 'But she won't be home for a while yet and we'll have got a head start. Besides, she won't know where the ceremony is to take place. It sure isn't in Lexington.'

Shade's silver-grey Chevrolet came roaring up the drive and Elgiva darted out into the hall. Following, Gemma noticed two suitcases standing at the foot of the stairs.

Elgiva pulled open the door as Todd Ives jumped out of the car and came bounding up the steps. Gemma saw that he had his dark suit on again and she guessed he was to be best man at the ceremony.

He stopped dead at the sight of Elgiva and swept off his smart new stetson, giving her a look of frank appraisal. 'You sure look great!' He noticed Gemma and a puzzled frown creased his brow.

'She knows,' said Elgiva. 'It can't be helped.'

Todd came into the hall and picked up the two suitcases.

'Hurry!' begged Elgiva. 'Gran said she'll shoot you the next time you set foot in this house.'

'I wish you'd reconsider,' said Gemma, standing on the top step. 'Can't you say something to her, Todd?'

He gave one of his noncommittal shrugs. 'I wouldn't like to interfere, miss.'

Surprisingly, Elgiva placed a hand on Gemma's sleeve and kissed her cheek. 'It'll be all right. Have faith!'

With that she ran down the steps and climbed into the front seat of the Chevrolet. The car slid forward, gathering speed until it disappeared from sight behind the trees.

A quarter of an hour later Gemma, standing anxiously in the drawing-room window, caught sight of Mrs Prescott's Lincoln car coming along the drive; Yarwood had refused to drive the Cadillac until it had been repaired.

Gemma rushed to the front door to confront Mrs Prescott with the news. 'Elgiva's marrying Shade today. Todd Ives came for her. I gather the ceremony's to be out of town somewhere.'

'No!' gasped Mrs Prescott, paling. 'But why? I don't understand. She knows I approve of Shade.' She turned to the housekeeper. 'Quickly, Vikki, go up to Elgiva's room and see if there's anything that will give us a clue as to where the wedding is to take place.'

Gemma took the old lady's arm and led her into the drawing-room. After settling her in an armchair she went to the cocktail cabinet and poured a stiff drink.

'Thank you, Gemma, I really needed that.' Mrs Prescott's eyes hardened. 'That ungrateful little witch! I've done everything for her and this is the way she repays me. I mean to stop this wedding, Gemma. I won't have her treating me in this way.'

'Perhaps you could call the police . . . have them look out . . .' suggested Gemma.

'No! No cops,' cried Mrs Prescott. 'I don't need that kind of publicity. What will people think? Going off and marrying in this hole-in-the-corner way!'

Vikki arrived with a small writing pad and thrust it into Mrs Prescott's hand. 'It just says "22nd May, 1.30. See to licence and blood tests".'

Mrs Prescott thought rapidly. 'Gemma, ring Shade's mother. She might know something about this. And if she doesn't she should be informed!'

Gemma spoke to the secretary at Five Oaks and discovered that Mrs Lambert was away in Florida. However,
Shade had left a message on the office dictaphone that he
had gone to Carolville on a personal matter.

'That's a village about a hundred miles to the south
of here,' said Mrs Prescott, 'just this side of Bowling
Green. It's a favourite place for weddings, in the
Mammoth Cave National Park area.' She slapped her
thigh excitedly. 'Now I come to think of it, Todd Ives
has an uncle who's a minister in Carolville. Todd
probably helped them arrange the wedding. Trust him
to be involved! Gemma, ring up the information bureau
and find out the name of Mr Ives' chapel.'

Minutes later Gemma had the information. 'The
Chapel of the White Lilacs,' she said.

Mrs Prescott struggled out of her chair. 'Right, I'm
stopping this wedding. She can't treat me like this. I'll
force her to come home and get married in the decent
way. Vikki, go and get the Cadillac . . .'

'But Yarwood's taking it in to Lexington for repairs
this afternoon . . .' began Vikki.

'Never mind about that,' snapped Mrs Prescott. 'Tell
him I need it. You can drive, Vikki. The less Yarwood
and the servants know about this the better.'

'But they have a half an hour start on us,' Vikki
pointed out. 'We'll never get to Carolville by one-thirty.
It's noon now!'

'Oh yes, we will!' Mrs Prescott knocked back the rest
of her drink. 'The Cadillac travels faster than a Chevy.
You come too, Gemma. I've a feeling I shall need your
support.'

Gemma's heart sank. She had no wish to gatecrash
Shade's wedding, nor to see Elgiva humiliated if Mrs
Prescott made a scene.

The three of them piled into the Cadillac, Vikki driving, Gemma sitting with Mrs Prescott in the back.

'Can you arrange a wedding so quickly?' asked

Gemma as they drove out of the gates. 'In England it takes three weeks.'

'You only need three days in this state,' said Mrs Prescott. 'They must have arranged it when they were away those two days.' She rapped on the dividing window with her stick and Vikki wound down the glass. 'Drive faster, Vikki, there's little traffic about.'

'May I remind you that the speed limit is fifty-five miles an hour!' said the housekeeper irritably. 'Do you want me to break it?'

'Yes, I do! I'll take the consequences,' declared Mrs Prescott. 'We must get there in time to stop the wedding.'

'How can you stop it?' asked Vikki. 'Elgiva is eighteen years old . . .'

'If all else fails I'll bribe the minister,' said Mrs Prescott maliciously. 'If he's an Ives then it should be easy!' She fell back against the seat, overcome by despair. 'I love that girl. Oh, why has she gone about things in this underhanded manner? I wanted to give her a splendid send-off—invite all my friends, have all the trimmings.'

'Perhaps she doesn't want that,' said Gemma kindly. 'Perhaps the very idea scares her.'

'Nonsense!' said Mrs Prescott. 'The girl's a born show-off. She'd love it.'

'Have you thought that there might be another reason?' said Vikki over her shoulder. 'That she might be pregnant?'

Mrs Prescott digested this suggestion for a moment, her mouth set in a firm line. 'If she is then we can hold the wedding soon, next week. A quiet affair.'

They reached Carolville, a quiet village in the heart of the National Park. There were several wedding chapels, and at last they located the Chapel of the White Lilacs, a pretty little brick building in a peaceful tree-lined street.

'There, we made it with five minutes to spare,' said Mrs Prescott triumphantly.

'It still may not be the place,' said Vikki. 'That message Shade left may have been a red herring.'

'No, this is the place, I'm sure of it.' Mrs Prescott peered out of the window and pointed to the side of the chapel. 'There's the Chevrolet, and Shade's Porsche next to it.'

Gemma glanced at the two cars and a feeling of utter misery engulfed her.

Mrs Prescott alighted and studied the notice board outside the chapel. It read: Minister—The Reverend Marcus Ives.

'Glad I remembered Todd's uncle was in this wedding racket,' snorted Mrs Prescott. 'The nerve of him! I bet he took great satisfaction arranging this secret shindig. Well, we'll see about that!'

She stormed up the steps, followed by Gemma and Vikki, and pushed open the door.

At once they were in a sparsely furnished hall. The only occupant was Shade Lambert, very casually dressed and smoking a cigarette. He looked startled to see them.

'Henrietta!' He kissed the old lady's cheek and glanced over her shoulder at the others. 'How did you . . .?'

She pulled away from him angrily. 'Don't you soft-soap me! Where is she? Where's that ungrateful grand-daughter of mine?'

Shade's expression was unreadable as he stubbed out the cigarette in an ashtray and half-turned to open a side door. It led to a kind of waiting-room, and standing in the centre were Elgiva and Todd Ives wrapped in each other's arms.

The silence was oppressive as the little group in the hall and the two people in the waiting-room exchanged amazed glances. Gemma was reminded of one of the silent tableaux at the recent pageant.

Mrs Prescott was the first to recover from her surprise. 'Todd Ives! What's the meaning of this?' She moved across the threshold, lifting her stick as if to strike the young man. 'Take your hands off her!'

Shade stepped forward and firmly took the stick from the old lady's hand, then restrained her further by putting his arms about her. 'Henrietta! They're in love.'

'I need to sit down,' said Mrs Prescott, passing a weary hand across her brow.

Vikka brought over a high-backed Windsor chair and Shade gently lowered the old lady into it.

Gemma's thoughts were thrown into chaos. She just could not cope with this turn of events. She gaped at Shade and, as if conscious of her gaze, he lifted his head to survey her until she was drowning in those amber pools.

'I don't understand any of this,' moaned Mrs Prescott. 'What's going on here? Elgiva, say something!'

Elgiva stared stubbornly at her grandmother and slipped her arm defiantly through Todd's.

'Calm down, Henrietta,' said Shade. 'These two young people want to get married, but they knew you'd never agree to it, so they've taken the law into their own hands. Can you blame them?'

'You mean you condone this deceitful behaviour?' demanded Mrs Prescott.

He ran his fingers through his hair. 'No, I don't condone it. I never even suspected it was on the cards. Todd promised me he'd leave it to me to talk you round.' He glanced disapprovingly at his farm foreman. 'I only realised what was up this morning from something one of my workers said. That's why I chased over here. Damned inconvenient it is too, when I'm having so much trouble with Cloud Pursued. I wanted to try to persuade them to postpone the ceremony until I'd had a chance to speak to you, but they wouldn't hear of it.'

'We'll see about that!' muttered Mrs Prescott darkly. She shot an angry glance in Elgiva's direction. 'You wicked girl! How could you? You hardly know the man!'

'You're wrong, Gran,' Elgiva cried passionately. 'I met him before you sent me away. We fell in love, but kept quiet about it because we knew you'd be angry. He's the reason I came home from Switzerland so soon. I couldn't bear to be apart from him any longer.'

So that was it, thought Gemma. But where did Shade come into all this?

As if in answer to her silent question, he said, 'I've deceived you, Henrietta. I saw no reason why Elgiva and Todd should be kept apart, so to save embarrassment all round and give them time to work things out, I let Elgiva pretend she was dating me.'

'Why, you snake in the grass, Shade Lambert!' declared the old lady. 'And I thought you were my friend!'

He laid a hand upon her shoulder and his features relaxed into a slow smile. 'I am your friend, Henrietta. But I'm Todd's friend too. I didn't want things to go this far without you knowing. I hate this elopement as much as you do, but there's nothing anyone can do. They're of marriageable age, they have the licence and the blood tests, you might as well accept the fact.'

'Bah!' retorted Mrs Prescott.

Elgiva stripped off her white gloves and, smiling tentatively, crossed the room to her grandmother. 'Our love has survived a long separation. We've written to each other constantly. And Todd flew out to Switzerland to be with me at Christmas. Can't you understand, Gran? I love him!'

'It's the real thing all right,' commented Shade cryptically, glancing briefly at Gemma.

She struggled inwardly to ignore the uncomfortable sensation his look aroused in her.

'Listen, Henrietta,' he said, taking a chair and sitting close to Mrs Prescott. 'Your Wayne and Quincey Ives had a difference of opinion and finished up hating one another. That's old history now. It has nothing to do with Elgiva and Todd.'

'That's right,' said Todd, speaking for the first time since they had arrived. 'Won't you give us your blessing?' He met the old lady's gaze steadfastly. 'Because we intend to wed with it or without it.'

Someone coughed outside the open door and they observed the minister standing there regarding them. 'I heard raised voices,' he said in way of explanation for his sudden appearance.

Mrs Prescott took her stick from Shade and dug it into the carpet, as she struggled to her feet. 'So you're Marcus Ives? You look mighty like your brother.'

'Yes, people used to remark upon the likeness,' said the minister. 'And you must be Mrs Prescott.' He grimaced good humouredly. 'I sure have heard a lot about you!'

A plump elderly woman, whom Gemma took to be the minister's wife, hovered in the doorway. 'Ready when you are,' she announced cheerfully.

Elgiva tucked her arm through Todd's again and eyed her grandmother challengingly. 'Well, Gran, are you coming to my wedding or aren't you?'

The old lady held her breath for a moment, then expelled it in a long sigh. 'Looks like I've got no option.'

Elgiva swiftly kissed her grandmother's cheek. 'I love you, Gran.'

'I wanted you to have a swell wedding,' moaned Mrs Prescott as they all went across the hall into the chapel.

It was a pleasant room, Gemma observed, with a small cloth-covered altar and rows of spindly chairs. Vases of flowers crowded the windowsills, their heady perfume pervading the room.

As the group took up their traditional positions, Gemma reflected that, apart from the bride and groom, they were hardly dressed for a wedding. Shade wore a tee-shirt, sports jacket and slacks. Mrs Prescott and Vikki still wore the simple cotton dresses in which they had gone shopping that morning. Gemma herself wore a faded denim working dress.

Both Elgiva and Todd gave their responses in strong clear tones and Mrs Prescott, still looking dazed, shed a few tears.

'Will you be a witness, Shade?' asked Todd, after they were pronounced man and wife.

'Yes, you and Gemma,' breathed Elgiva, smiling enigmatically.

The register was brought and the bride and groom duly signed. Then Shade picked up the pen and handed it to Gemma. He stood very close to her, breathing down her neck, as she signed in a shaky scrawl, then he added his own signature with a bold flourish.

Todd pulled Elgiva into his arms and kissed her, then turned to Mrs Prescott and, taking both her hands in his, gently kissed her cheek.

She sniffed again and rummaged in her bag for her handkerchief.

Suddenly everyone was kissing everyone else. Gemma reeled under the force of it all. She felt Todd's shaggy red moustache tickle her nose, had the breath squeezed out of her from the minister's hug, and trembled as Shade's lips brushed her cheek.

'Now for the wedding breakfast,' said Mrs Prescott. 'I noticed quite a passable restaurant in the village as we came through.' She held up her hand as Elgiva and Todd began to protest. 'You did me out of the preparations, don't do me out of the wedding breakfast. You and your wife are invited too, Reverend.'

The young couple gave in gracefully and everyone went outside to the cars.

Shade eyed the dent in the Cadillac's door. 'How did that happen?'

'Gemma did that,' giggled Vikki. 'On the way back from Buffalo. She was a little upset about something.'

Gemma turned her head away, unable to meet Shade's enquiring eyes.

They removed themselves to a modern restaurant in the main square where Mrs Prescott demanded a table for eight and ordered a four-course meal along with four bottles of Bollinger champagne. She even managed to coax from the proprietor a single-tiered iced cake which he had been preparing for a party to be held there the following day. The fact that it was pink and decorated with the words 'Happy Birthday, Lindy' did not seem to matter.

'I hope you've thought this all out,' said Mrs Prescott. 'Where are you going to live?'

'Todd's found an apartment in Lexington,' said Elgiva. 'It's expensive, but I expect to become a fully fledged stenographer when my course is finished in July. I'll soon get a job.'

'You'll do no such thing,' drawled Todd.

Elgiva gazed adoringly at her new husband. 'Isn't he masterful? A real male chauvinist! I must work, darling. I'll be bored to death doing nothing. Besides, Gran's bound to cut me off without a cent.'

'Don't be silly, child,' said Mrs Prescott. 'Only don't count on collecting yet. I intend living to be a hundred.'

'I'll keep my own wife, thank you,' said Todd. He added, with a touch of humour, 'Of course if she wants to go out to work for pin money then that's her affair. But after I've given her a couple of kids she won't find time hanging so heavily on her hands.'

Mrs Prescott looked quickly from one to the other of them and Elgiva laughed suddenly.

'No, Gran, we didn't *have* to get married,' she said. 'Despite your opinion of young people today, Todd and I have not 'misbehaved' ourselves. You can thank him for that. He knew you had a down on him and didn't want to sink any lower in your estimation.'

'What about the other night?' asked Mrs Prescott acidly, as a thought occurred to her. 'Todd was coming out of your room when Gemma found him in the corridor, wasn't he? You'd both sneaked indoors!'

Gemma caught her breath as everything became clear—the car in the courtyard after the party, the prowler on the lawn, Elgiva's visits to Five Oaks, her vain attempt to give Todd her favour at the steeplechase . . .

Todd grinned apologetically at Gemma. 'Sorry I had to string you along the other night.'

Elgiva's cheeks grew pink. 'Even then we . . . didn't . . . It was that night we decided to get married before our feelings ran away with us. At least Todd decided.'

That would account for the look of ecstasy on Todd's face when she'd caught him in the corridor, thought Gemma.

'So you see he's behaved impeccably,' finished Elgiva.

'Has he?' asked Shade wryly. 'I wish he'd waited till the foaling season was over. Now I expect he'll demand time off for a honeymoon just when I need him at the farm.'

Elgiva leaned across the table and stroked Shade's hand. 'My need is greater! Just a couple of days, eh, Shade honey?'

'But you've just had a couple of days!' he growled.

'I know. We went up to Boston to see Todd's mother and get her blessing,' said Elgiva. 'She's an invalid or she would have been here today.'

'Okay,' sighed Shade. 'Can't see how I can refuse.'

Mrs Prescott sent out for a photographer and when the man arrived the party moved to the sunlit terrace to record the occasion for the family album.

'That appears to be that,' said Shade to Gemma as they stood side by side in the shadow of a leafy crabapple tree.

He seemed so distant, she thought. This was the first time he had addressed her directly.

'I suppose so,' she said slowly. Her thoughts were running wild. Why hadn't he told her? Why had he let her go on thinking he was in love with Elgiva? And then she remembered—he *had* told her, time and again. Only she had chosen to believe Elgiva.

The silence between them became embarrassing. Gemma watched him take out a Camel cigarette and light it. 'I thought you didn't smoke.'

'I've had a lot on my mind lately.' He glanced impatiently at his watch. 'I can't hang around here any longer,' he said bluntly. 'I'm needed at Five Oaks.'

He nodded curtly to her then went to make his apologies to Mrs Prescott.

After he had gone the rest of them walked to the little post office to send a cable to Elgiva's mother in Argentina. Then the newlyweds climbed into the Chevrolet.

Just before they drove off, Elgiva leaned out of the window and said to Gemma, 'Sorry I had to deceive you, but everything will be okay now. Didn't I tell you so?'

Gemma pondered these words all the way home in the Cadillac. How little Elgiva knew! When it had first sunk into Gemma's brain that Shade was not marrying Elgiva after all, for wild moments she had thought that the way was now clear for them to get together, but calm reasoning brought home to her the fact that things were now a thousandfold worse.

All the time Gemma had been able to tell herself Shade had rejected her at the cottage because he loved another, she had been able to hold on to her pride with some vestige of dignity. Even telling herself that he might have rejected her out of some respect for her did not offer any consolation. A man like Shade? And if that were the case—if he had suddenly been overcome by an attack of conscience—then why that bruising kiss in the library? And why no word from him since? Ten days had passed. The answer was simple. He had thrown her aside because he was not attracted to her! He had deliberately set out to make her fall for him but, despite all his compliments, when he had had the opportunity to make love to her, he had opted out! Today when he didn't have to pretend to anyone that he was dating Elgiva, he had declined to show any interest in Gemma whatsoever.

She had to face it. Shade had finished with her! Perhaps it was just as well. What had he said? 'You're out of your league'. How pertinent those words appeared now!

The next day passed uneventfully. Gemma accompanied Mrs Prescott on a prize-giving visit to a local school and helped to entertain a Congressman and his wife to dinner in the evening.

A parcel arrived for Gemma the following morning and the maid brought it to the apartment. It bore a local postmark and Gemma's first thought was that it was from Shade. He was getting in touch with her after all! She tore eagerly at the wrappings and found the jade pendant duly repaired. She burst into tears.

She sat forlornly on the bed, allowing the necklace to weigh heavily in her hand. Guilt and anguish clouded her conscience. She hadn't given Rowan a thought for days, and never would again—not in that same special way. For the world had moved on apace and she could no longer gain any comfort from his memory.

She glanced at his photograph, then placed it together with the pendant in the bottom drawer of her dressing table.

She thought vaguely of giving in her notice and catching the first available flight home, but the thought of having to face her mother and sister after only two months away galled her. They were well-meaning, but they would stifle her with their concern as they had before. And she would be the laughing-stock of the village. Straightening, she took a deep breath. She must pick up the threads of her life and stop feeling sorry for herself. Beginning now! With this resolve she went downstairs.

She had just opened the morning's mail and stepped to the window to adjust the blinds against the brightness of the sun, when she saw the Porsche standing in the courtyard outside her office. Her stomach twisted into a familiar knot of wretchedness before she forced herself to relax. She would have to get used to Shade calling to see Mrs Prescott from time to time.

She jumped as there came a rap on the door and it opened to reveal Shade, dressed in a bush jacket and old corduroy trousers. He eyed her tentatively. 'Hi!'

'If you're looking for Mrs Prescott ...' she said quickly.

'I'm not.' He laid a small spray of gardenias on the desk. Gemma's gaze flickered from the flowers to his face. What was he up to now? she wondered suspiciously. She was not going to fall for any of his tricks again, so he needn't think she was.

'I've been up all night.' He yawned and ruffled his fingers through his hair. His face did look haggard, but she noted that he had taken the trouble to shave.

'Then shouldn't you be home in bed right now?'

He ignored her sarcasm. 'My mare Cloud Pursued has produced the prettiest filly you ever did see. It'll be a champion for sure.'

Gemma could not help sharing his relief at the safe delivery of the foal after so much worry. 'Oh, I'm so pleased!'

He hadn't expected her to say that and an unguarded expression crossed his features. For a moment his air of self-assurance seemed to have deserted him. A heavy silence hung over the room, then he said, 'Would you like to come over and see the new filly?'

'No, I'm busy.'

'She's a light chestnut colour with blonde mane and tail,' he went on, undeterred. 'I'm going to call her Fair English Maid after you.'

Gemma gasped audibly and was at a loss for words. Then she sniffed disparagingly. 'Really?' Oh no, she wasn't going to fall for his tricks again.

'Gemma!'

Her shoulders drooped. 'Leave me alone,' she pleaded wearily. 'I can't take any more.'

'I need to talk to you,' he said urgently.

'No! Go away!'

'I've been working things out.'

'Things?' She was curious despite her resolve to have nothing more to do with him. 'What things?'

'Us.'

She trembled violently, then gave a derisive laugh. 'Huh!'

Shade shrugged negligently and tried a different tack. Looking at the neat pile of lists on the desk—the first batch of Gemma's library cataloguing—he exclaimed, 'You've worked wonders here. Mrs Prescott is very pleased with you.'

'Does that surprise you?' Her eyes flew wide open. 'Didn't you expect me to be able to do the job when you engaged me?'

He laughed uncomfortably. 'Haven't you ever wondered how you got the position of companion/ secretary to Mrs Prescott?'

She didn't like the way this conversation was going. She summoned every ounce of poise she possessed to say blithely, 'Often!'

'Oh yes, you were in the final twelve applicants,' he went on reflectively. 'But your qualifications weren't all that outstanding.' Gemma gaped at him. He caught her chin between his strong fingers and she detected the faint smell of horse liniment. 'Your typing and shorthand speeds were pretty average, and you had no experience of being a companion. When I fed everything into the computer you came seventh. Even that silly vain redhead beat you.'

She shook her chin free from his hand. 'Thanks a lot!'

He frowned. 'And you were very rude to me!'

She glared at him. 'You asked for it!'

Shade threaded his fingers into her hair, then tightened his grip and drew her gently towards him. 'All the other applicants were falling over themselves to be nice to me, but not you.'

She swallowed hard, wondering what all this plain speaking was leading up to. 'Let me go!' In vain she tried to free her hair, but only succeeded in bringing pain to her tender roots.

'The reason I chose you for the job was because you presented a challenge to my male ego.'

Their faces were inches apart. She curled her lip contemptuously and snapped, 'You think I haven't worked that one out?'

'I see!' He let go of her hair and seized her upper arms. 'Well, hear this! Once I'd gotten you out here I intended to seduce you!'

'Why didn't you, then?' Her outspokenness surprised her. 'You had the chance!'

It was his turn to stare open-mouthed and the pressure on her arms increased. She lifted her foot with the intention of kicking him on the shin, but he sidestepped neatly.

'Hold still, you little wildcat!' he cried.

'So you can tell me how stupid I've been?'

He gave her a little shake. 'Let me finish. I intended to get you into bed.' His hands fell away from her. 'End of plan!' Gemma rubbed her limbs where his fingers had dug into the flesh. His voice became husky. 'But somewhere along the way I fell in love with you.'

She looked at him quickly, hardly daring to breathe. 'Fell in love with me?' she repeated, stupefied.

He laid a hand against her neck, then allowed his forefinger to trail over her cheekbone and into the little hollow beside her mouth, wreaking havoc to her self-control. 'I was too insensitive to realise what had happened to me,' he whispered. 'When you declared your love for me at the cottage, you threw me right off balance. I suddenly realised my motives had changed. It wasn't a game any more. I couldn't get out of that bedroom fast enough.'

'I got that impression,' she said bitterly.

'I know. I'm sorry. I refused to accept that I was in love with you.' He laughed scornfully. 'Me! The guy who was above all that mush! That kiss in the library afterwards ... I wanted to punish you for what you'd done to me! I thought that if I left you alone after that I'd get over it.' His finger pursued its exploration of her lips. 'Some hopes!'

Gemma smoothed the lapels of his bush jacket, then, because he looked so wretched and less confident than she had ever seen him, she stood on tiptoe and feathered a forgiving kiss against his cheek.

He took heart from her gesture and his hands claimed her waist. 'It's twelve days since I left Buffalo. The worst twelve days of my life! I ... I never knew what the real thing was.'

So he'd been counting too. 'Neither did I,' she murmured.

'You mean ...?'

'I had no idea what the real thing was until I met you,' she told him with unashamed frankness.

An expression of wonder filled his eyes. 'Are you saying you still love me, after the way I treated you?'

'Yes, I still love you.'

'That's all I wanted to know.' He crushed his mouth to hers with that old mastery she remembered so well, awakening in her a deep physical desire.

They surfaced for air and Shade cradled her head in his hands, examining her face as if seeing her for the first time and wanting to memorise every detail of her features.

Gemma basked in the glow of his admiration and saw that the passion burning in his amber eyes was tightly controlled.

'Gemma,' he said at last, his voice deep with emotion, 'will you marry me?'

A trembling sigh escaped her. 'Yes, Shade.'

They lost all account of time in the next spate of kisses.

'You're tired,' she said softly, as he dropped into the office chair and pulled her on to his lap.

'No, I'm not tired any more. Your answer has revitalised me.' He buried her face against his throat and she felt his vocal cords throb as he chuckled, 'It feels kinda strange.'

'Hm?' she murmured.

'Being engaged to be married.'

She moved her head to his shoulder and smiled up at him. 'Having doubts already?'

'Doubts? Never!' His lips nuzzled her cheek. 'Proposing to you was just about *the* smartest thing I've ever done. And your acceptance was something akin to a miracle.'

A feeling of contentment invaded her body and, she ran her finger under his smooth chin. 'Elgiva said the most wonderful thing in the world is when the person you love loves you.'

'Wise beyond her years, that one,' said Shade. He bestowed a kiss of infinite tenderness on Gemma's lips. 'You know, the darnedest thing is that I fell in love with you at our first meeting, back in London. Since then I haven't been interested in other women.'

'Oh, come!' she mocked him gently.

But it rang true. Those elegant women at the Kentucky Derby. 'Shade, sugar-pie, long time no see!'

'What about the redhead . . . and the brunette at the theatre?'

'I know you won't believe this, but the redhead got no satisfaction that evening. I think I bored her. Is it any wonder, when thoughts of you were running through my mind? And Miranda, the brunette, really is my cousin. I'll invite her to the wedding and prove it.'

'Mrs Prescott, Vikki and the Judge all said you were a lady-killer,' she teased him. 'You may revert to type after we're married, and I don't think I'd like that.'

He snorted derisively. 'There have been women, I can't deny it, but don't believe everything you hear. A thirty-year-old bachelor is expected to have a certain reputation. Mine is vastly exaggerated and it sure is hell to live up to. I'm looking forward to devoting the rest of my life to you, my sweet.' He kissed her nose and gently pushed her from his lap. 'Come on, I want you to see the new filly taking her first faltering steps. Did I tell you? I'm giving her to you as a wedding present.'

Gemma's eyes shone. 'Oh, Shade!' She picked up the gardenias and buried her nose in them.

He took a half-smoked packet of cigarettes from his pocket, crushed them and dropped them ceremoniously into the waste bin. Then he propelled her towards the door. 'First we must tell Henrietta our news.'

Gemma's hand flew to her mouth. 'Whatever will she say?'

'I suppose I'll have to charm her round.' He winked. 'If that's okay with you. I can offer to send to England for a replacement companion/secretary. The redhead, maybe!' He saw Gemma bristle. 'No, maybe not!'

They walked along the corridor hand in hand. 'Shall we apply for the licence today?' Shade asked. 'It takes three days...'

'Hold on!' she gasped. 'I must send for my mother and sister . . .'

He shrugged resignedly. 'Okay. But we won't wait too long, will we? Those cold showers are murder.'

'No, we won't wait too long,' she agreed.

He hugged her close as they paused outside the drawing-room door. 'The real thing turns out to be pretty wonderful, Gemma.'

She sighed. 'Hm, doesn't it?'

Harlequin Plus

YOU'RE A WHAT?

Harlequin books are set all over the world, and we have found it sometimes interesting to note what inhabitants of certain cities and countries are called. Following are just a few our editors have come across in their travels through Harlequin Romances and Presents.

Place	Inhabitant
Aberdeen	Aberdonian
Belgium (northern)	Fleming
Belgium (southern)	Walloon
Birmingham	Brummagem or Brummer
Cambridge, Mass.	Cantabrigian
Florence	Florentine
Frankfurt	Frankfurter
Glasgow	Glaswegian
Halifax	Haligonian
Hamburg	Hamburger
Isle of Orkney	Arcadian
Liverpool	Liverpudlian
Madagascar	Malagasy
Madrid	Madrilenian
Manchester	Mancunian
Moscow	Muscovite
Nice	Niçois
Newcastle	Novocastrian
Norfolk and Suffolk	East Anglian
Palermo	Palermitan
Seattle	Seattleite
Venice	Venetian

There are many more such unusual names, of course—far more than we can list here. Watch for them in a future "Plus"!

PASSIONATE!
CAPTIVATING!
SOPHISTICATED!

Harlequin Presents.

**The favorite fiction
of women the world over!**

Beautiful contemporary romances that
touch every emotion of a woman's heart-
passion and joy, jealousy and heartache...
but most of all...love.

Fascinating settings in the exotic
reaches of the world—
from the bustle of an international capital
to the paradise of a tropical island.

**All this and much, much more
in the pages of**

Harlequin Presents...

**Wherever paperback books are sold, or through
Harlequin Reader Service**

In the U.S.
1440 South Priest Drive
Tempe, AZ 85281

In Canada
649 Ontario Street
Stratford, Ontario N5A 6W

**No one touches the heart of a woman
quite like Harlequin!**